Foodprints

A Trail of Food and Memories

Priya Bala

Popular Prakashan
www.popularprakashan.com

Published by
Harsha Bhatkal for
POPULAR PRAKASHAN PVT. LTD.
301, Mahalaxmi Chambers
22, Bhulabhai Desai Road
Mumbai – 400 026
www.popularprakashan.com

First Published 2014

(4381)
ISBN: 978-81-7991-821-0

Cover: Gaman Palem
Illustration: Padmini Sivarajah
Layout: Anjali Sawant

Printed in India
by Repro India Ltd.
Navi Mumbai - 400 710

Tribute

This is for my mother, who kindled in me the love of good food and endowed me with a flair for cooking. When I told her about the idea of this book, she was all enthusiasm, as she was about most things. I discussed with her the recipes I should include, asked her for tips and wrote down the ingredients for her famous-in-our-circles curry powder. She passed away in May 2011, before I could complete this book. This is another of those many things I should have done when she was there to see and celebrate it.

And celebrate life is what she did till her last day. The nurturing of home and family – and ours went far beyond the nuclear – were key to her everyday happiness.

She was a superlative cook who turned out the daily meals with the same passion that she did her special treats. I remember the packed lunches she would send to school for me, the colourful tid-bits she would carefully craft for our birthday parties and the elaborate dinners she served. She stayed at it through the years, doing the same for her grandchildren, sending spice powders and packed foods for my brother and family who live abroad and cooking food for all those in her care.

Her circle of nurturing extended far beyond her immediate family. She would visit sick friends and expectant mothers carrying food. Even those who came to work at home, a carpenter or gardener, could always expect a warm, fresh meal.

The resources for such generosity were sometimes stretched. My family has seen more upheavals than most. My mother braved it all, including the consequences of my youthful follies. She was resilient, positive, optimistic and did everything in her power to keep the show going and everyone well-fed and nourished.

Her legacy to me is not that of being an efficient and enthusiastic cook. It is the philosophy that you must give and give generously, and that food is one such simple gift.

About This Book

Food memories are among the best. Remember the taste of your seventh birthday cake? Or the first time you ate pizza? The comforting feel of the sambar and rice your mother mixed and fed you?

I began this book in an attempt to put down and cherish my fondest memories of food. It has also become a tribute to everyone who created a great food moment for me – starting from my mother, who encouraged me to bake my first cake, to my friends both here and abroad who've introduced me to new cuisines, and the talented chefs who gave me gourmet experiences.

This is not only a thank you note, as it were, to all those who've accepted my meal invitations and enjoyed my food, it's also a collection of recipes of the food from the places I've been. Because I grew up in Sri Lanka, there are several stories about the food from the beautiful island.

There are dishes from my family home in Madurai; from my trips to Kolkata and from further away, such as the lovely champagne region in France, Australia and Morocco.

All the recipes in this book are dishes which I make frequently for my family and friends. I hope you will enjoy cooking with this book as much as I did writing it.

Contents

1 My First Butter Cake

It was a time when life didn't come fitted with gadgets. I remember the arrival of our telephone, the sort in which you dialled the numbers with your fingers in a groove. And oh the excitement of the first TV! Small, black and white, heavily pixelated and requiring the adjustment of an outdoor antenna while the rest of us yelled from inside, 'Right, right, just there, oh no it's gone again!' And thus we watched the serialised version of Anna Karenina, enraptured by the dark Count Vronsky.

Then came the fridge, calling for another celebration. We fell upon the bottles of cold water with glee and ate vast quantities of the ice cream my mother made with condensed milk. But we didn't have an oven for the longest time. We didn't do without cakes though.

The birthday cakes were ordered from one particular cake-maker, year after year. There was a crinoline lady for my sister's third birthday and a piano with the keys in white icing and dark chocolate for my ninth. The icing was all-butter with silver balls glistening on the rows of piped rosettes. But we had everyday cakes, too. Not every day, but as a special teatime treat on weekends. My mother and her sisters, one of who always lived with us, had just discovered they could bake cakes at home without a whole lot of equipment.

My mother was an adventurous cook and kept a thick notebook bursting with recipes cut out from newspapers and old issues of Femina, some of which I shall tell you about later. So, it's only natural she tried her hand at baking, butter cakes being a starting point. Well, they weren't always butter. Food shortages often left us to use Astra margarine; Australian butter was for special occasions. You creamed the margarine and sugar in a large bowl with a wooden spoon till your elbow came off, added flour and egg yolks alternately, and then folded in stiffly beaten whites.

A good lashing of grated lime zest and it was ready to be baked. There was no preheating, no oven temperature to be checked. Indeed, no oven as I told you. What the smart women of my family and their circle did was to pile clean sea sand onto a griddle – the one we used to make rotti, the recipe for which will come later – and place it over a flame to get really hot. They then poured the cake batter into a square or round biscuit tin, recycled to become bakeware, set the thing on the sand and allowed it to bake slowly. Sure it got a bit crusty in bits and some of it may have stuck to the biscuit tin, but eaten warm, smelling of the lime peel my mother always put in these cakes, they were amazingly good. When I first tried my hand at cooking at around eight years of age, baking this butter cake is one of the first things I did.

The cake, which I still feel inspired to bake when I have friends over on a Sunday afternoon, is derived very much from that. Only now, I use an electric oven and an electric mixer. I have a non-stick cake tin as well. But I always use my mother's lime zest.

Butter Cake

175 gm unsalted butter + for greasing

175 gm soft white sugar (run through the blender if it's too coarse)

3 eggs at room temperature

175 gm refined flour + for dusting

1 tsp baking powder

1 tbsp grated zest of lime

Preheat the oven to 170°C/325°F/Gas Mark 3. Prepare a nine-inch round cake tin; greasing it lightly with butter and then dusting with flour. To do this, sprinkle the buttered surface with a teaspoon or two of flour, shake the tin about so that the flour adheres to the tin.

Alternatively, use a lightly greased non-stick tin. Sift the flour and baking powder together. Put the butter which should be soft and at room temperature and the sugar into a large bowl and beat with an electric mixer till it's pale and fluffy.

Break the eggs in, one at a time, beating well after you add each. Shoot the flour in, along with the lime zest, mix briefly, pour into the prepared tin and bake for 30-35 minutes, by which time a toothpick inserted should come out clean. Allow to cool for half an hour and turn out. Don't fret, if some of it sticks. Just cut the rest into neat slices and serve.

Makes one 9-inch cake

For Fool-proof Cakes

Make sure the butter is at room temperature and soft. The eggs should always be at room temperature too.

2 The World's Best Fruit Cake, Really

If the butter cake in the preceding recipe is simplicity itself, then here is the ultimate tropical luxury in baking: the Sri Lankan Christmas cake. It is stuffed with fruit and nuts, which have been soaked for several hours in honey, rose water and brandy, the whole thing barely held together with semolina, not flour. It is aromatic with cardamom, cinnamon, cloves and nutmeg. For me, it brings back also the fragrance of Christmas in Colombo, that brief season when the oppressive heat gives way to a barely perceptible nip in the air. And the light changes.

That's when school would've closed for the year after the Christmas party. The fare at these class parties included Elephant House ice-cream in a mammoth styrofoam container, small fish cutlets and patties and coconut rock – each girl bringing a dish. And the class teacher gave us all gifts -- a pencil boxes, or Christmas crackers or hair clips. It was also the time when our vast household would empty.

All the cousins from the estates and other sundry relatives who stayed with us and studied went home for the holidays. So, it would be just my parents, and three of us kids. Every Christmas morning we went to the home of Reggie Michael, my father's editor, a tyrant at work, but the most genial host. Bubsy Aunty was an elegant woman, draped in chiffon, solitaires twinkling on earlobes and nostril and moving about in a waft of expensive perfume, the sort we never saw in imports-regulated Sri Lanka. Her dressing table was, to my young mind, a wonderland of rich lipsticks and coloured cosmetics. I would linger over it, touching things lovingly.

But best of all in the Michaels' effortlessly stylish home with its red floors polished to a shine, lovely old furniture and artefacts from their many travels abroad would be the Christmas cake. It was served in small squares, wrapped in gold foil and cellophane. That's also how they do it at weddings, for this is also the Sri Lankan wedding cake, covered with cashewnut marzipan and served in little paper boxes with the bride's and groom's names printed on it. I've eaten really good Christmas cake in many places, but nothing matches this. I've gathered many versions of the recipe, tweaked, experimented, baked and rebaked and come up with this version.

The list of ingredients is long, but once you get that bit out of the way, you can't go wrong. So bake a Lankan fruit cake this Christmas. It's never too early to start. In fact, it gets better with the keeping....

Christmas Cake

100 gm candied ginger	2 tsp ground cardamom
100 gm raisins	1 tsp ground cloves
300 gm sultanas	3 tbsp honey
100 gm currants	1 tbsp vanilla
200 gm candied ash gourd (*petha*)	1 wine glassful brandy
	3 tbsp rose water
200 gm cashew nuts	225 gm butter at room temperature
50 gm almonds	
100 gm glace cherries	225 gm semolina
½ nutmeg, grated	12 eggs
2 tsp ground cinnamon	400 gm soft brown sugar

Chop the fruit and nuts. Do not be tempted to put them in a mixer. The hand-chopped texture is all important. Place in a large glass bowl, add the ground spices and pour in the honey, vanilla, the brandy reserving 2 tablespoons for later use and rose water. Stir well and set aside to macerate for a day. Line two 8-inch cake tins with a double thickness of grease-proof paper. Preheat the oven to 150°C/300°F/Gas Mark 2.

Ensure the butter is at room temperature and soft. Place it in a large bowl and mix well with the semolina. Separate the eggs and beat the yolks with the sugar until pale and creamy. Add to the semolina-butter mixture. Stir in the soaked fruit and nuts and mix well. Now, whisk half the number of egg whites until stiff. (You can make meringues with the leftover egg whites - recipe on page 144).

Fold in the egg whites into the cake mixture a little at a time. Pour the batter into the two tins and cook for about 1½ hours, or until a skewer when inserted comes out clean. Cool the cake on a wire rack. Once cold, prick the surfaces with a skewer and pour one tablespoon of brandy over each cake. Cover with foil, place in an airtight tin. Do not be tempted to slice the cake for at least a fortnight.

Makes two 8-inch cakes

3 Chilled Chicks and Other Party Eats

I'm aware that birthday parties today are extravagant affairs, themed to a T and guaranteed to be every classmate's envy. So there are Barbie Doll bashes for the little princesses and Ben Ten big splashes for the boys.

Everything from the invitation cards to the return gifts are created around the theme and arranged by party organisers. When I was growing up, the birthday party was still a big deal, but everything was made at home. We had our birthday cakes ordered from a very accomplished cake-maker and the moment of its arrival would be one of much anticipation and excitement.

The rest of the party was pretty much home-style. At my place it was my Aunty Tonie who would be at the helm of affairs, drawing up a guest list, deciding on party decorations and, of course, the short-eats, which is how we referred to finger foods.

The women of my family were all skilled and talented cooks with endless enthusiasm for feeding a crowd. Party short-eats were different from anything else on the Sri Lankan table. The menu comprised about a dozen carefully crafted little morsels, especially designed to capture the imagination of children.

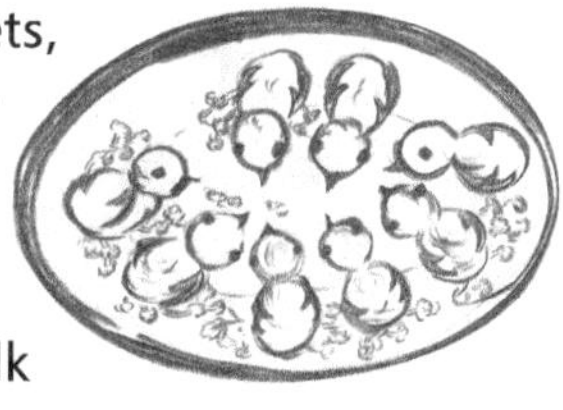

There would be little oval-shaped fish cutlets, with pastry necks stuck on, turning them into preening swans. Ribbon sandwiches were stacks of well butter bread, with beetroot, carrot and a green chutney filling. There were pinwheels, too. And fried bread circles piped with egg yolk and mayo to make basic canapés.

Cheeslings were assembled into little cottages, held together by date chutney. There were little flowerpots of carrot, filled with cream cheese and topped with a sprig of parsley, and tiny gougeres with a creamy filling.

There were the staples and also the innovations that would appear every year. One year, I remember, sandwich cutters were discovered and we had finger sandwiches that were heart-, club- and spade-shaped.

The odds and ends of bread were tossed in butter and popped into an oven to crisp up the next day. They were delicious.

And then one year my mother found a recipe for chilled chicks in *Femina*. If you have a toddler birthday party, your little guests will love these cute short-eats.

Chilled Chicks

500 gm floury potatoes
4 tbsp butter
Salt and pepper to taste
For the filling, a cup of cooked mince, chopped eggs or a medley of cooked and lightly mashed vegetables, well seasoned
12 cucumber slices
6 thin slices of carrot
12 tips of red chillies
24 peppercorns

Peel, cut and boil the potatoes till tender.

Mash till smooth, add the butter and adjust seasoning. Take about a tablespoon of mashed potato, form into a cup and place a little filling. Close up to make a ball.

Rest the ball on a cucumber slice. Make a smaller ball with the mashed potato, without filling and place to make a head for the chick. Use a carrot slice quarter each for wings, the chilli tip for a beak and two peppercorns for eyes.

Allow to chill and serve to the kiddies. Instruct them to remove the chillies and pepper before eating.

Makes 12 chilled chicks

4 A Simple Bread for Hungry Workers

There's always history in food. Not just Bearnaise sauce from the French courts and Gilawati kebabs from the kitchens of the Nawabs, but even the humble foods that hungry workers eat everywhere.

The rotti from Sri Lanka, not to be confused with the rather more refined roti of North India, is such a little wheel of history. If the migrant workers from India who went to work in the Caribbean combined cooking styles they were acquainted with and the ingredients of their new home to come up with dal-puri and doubles, the rotti was created from a sense of wonderment.

Migrant labour from the arid, southern districts of Tamil Nadu, who were grateful for a bowl of kanji or gruel, found themselves endowed with new rations on the tea estates of Sri Lanka where they arrived at the turn of the last century.

There was white, refined flour, known there as American flour, and coconuts which were a luxury ingredient. How did the women who worked the tea plantations come to combine the two, we do not know. But what emerged was a robust, tasty bread that had the advantage of keeping hunger at bay for hours; a crucial consideration for workers who toiled in rough weather and rougher terrain.

Of course, this simple bread has now moved from the line room kitchens and into urban homes. I'm often happy to serve it to guests with spicy curries and sambols as accompaniments.

The smell of baking rotti always reminds me of mist-clad tea estates and those hardy women whose fingers skim across the surface of tea bushes, tossing tea leaf buds into their baskets which grow heavier by the hour.

Rotti

2 cups refined flour

½ tsp salt

1 cup freshly grated coconut

Sift the flour into a wide bowl. Add the salt and the coconut and mix in. Now pour in 1 cup of warm water and bring the ingredients together. Knead for ten minutes till you have a soft, pliable dough.

Divide the dough into two portions and shape into balls. You can now press these onto a hot tawa to make the rotti. But novices may wish to use a board and rolling pin. Roll out the dough to a disc that's about half an inch thick.

Place it on a hot, lightly greased tawa, and cook pressing it down with a rolled up kitchen cloth and turning over frequently. Ensure the tawa stays at medium temperature – neither too hot which will cause the rotti to burn before it is cooked through, nor not hot enough which will result in an underbaked rotti.

When done, the rotti should be covered with gold-brown specks. While it's traditional to eat it with a Seeni Sambol (page 50), some butter melting over the hot rotti makes for a wonderful treat as well.

Makes 2 rotti

While Kneading Flour

Whether it's for rotti, chapati or for yeast breads, always use a large, roomy pan for kneading flour. It not only prevents any spills and mess, it allows you to knead well and freely.

5 Treats on a Tea Estate

When I was in school, holidays meant taking the first train out into the hill country. You left the warm and humid coast, travelled through the plains and then hit the mountains.

First the gentle slopes of Kandy and Gampola and then the high peaks. The train journey was a delight, the steam engines huffing up steep slopes, traversing hillsides clad in the green velvet of tea leaves. Streams gushed down the sides of rocks and occasionally there would be the drama of a roaring waterfall.

I have seen the Swiss Alps and other beautiful places. But up-country in Sri Lanka has a riveting beauty not easily rivalled. There, on an enchanting estate called Galaboda, my aunt – my mother's sister -- lived with her tea-maker husband, in a little stone cottage, facing the toytown railway station and with huge rocks surrounding it.

Here, the holiday weeks would pass, as we sunned ourselves on the rocks, frolicked in the garden with its blossoms of dahlia and fragrant gardenia, took long walks uphill to the homes of other estate staff, read, all cosy under warm clothes in the cold nights, and ate some of the best food of my childhood.

Sinnamma kept cows. I loved milk with cream floating on top and would drink a big glass every morning, in the warm kitchen with a chunk of kitul jaggery for sweetness. For breakfast she made crisp Rotti (page 18) and Seeni Sambol (page 50), ground on a stone, or Puttu (page 38) from roasted refined flour, steamed in a length of bamboo and served with coconut milk. Ah, the joys of comfort food!

And because we were on holiday, running about the estate, we were always hungry. Besides the hearty breakfasts, lunches and dinners, there were special teatime treats. No junk food from packets or paper tubs, but wholesome, homemade things.

On some days, patties with a filling of spicy tinned fish and potato, squares of coconut rock when we were in the mood for something sweet and, frequently, something as simple and earthy as susiyam.

It is merely batter-fried balls of cooked green gram mashed with coconut and sugar. Do not scoff at its simplicity. Served with the love of an aunt, who was as dear to me as my mother, they were little globes of happiness.

Susiyam

1 cup whole green gram	A pinch of turmeric powder
1 cup caster sugar	A pinch of salt
1 cup freshly grated coconut	Oil for deep-frying
1 cup refined flour	

Soak the green gram for about six hours and pressure-cook till tender, but not mushy.

One whistle should do. Drain and set aside. The stock makes a very nice rasam. Allow the cooked gram to cool and then mash gently with the back of a ladle. Add the sugar and grated coconut. Form into small lime-sized balls. Set aside.

Whisk about half a cup water into the refined flour, to make a thick, smooth batter. Add the turmeric powder and salt and stir well. Heat the oil in a thick-bottomed karhai.

Dip the gram balls carefully in the batter, slip into the oil and deep-fry till golden yellow. Eat warm.

Every time I do, I am back in my childhood, when I played all day and rushed home for a sweet teatime treat.

Makes 12 susiyam

6 Rice for Auspicious Days

This is Sri Lanka's favourite breakfast rice. Yes, no one looks askance at eating rice thrice a day in the paddy-growing island. Milk rice or kiribath is also a rice for special occasions such as the Sinhala New Year.

The end of the old year is marked by an all-round shutting down. It's not just shops and businesses, kitchens in homes shut down as well. And then, at an appointed hour, the new hearth is lit and the milk rice is cooked to signal an auspicious beginning.

It is not unlike the pongal of Tamil Nadu, except that it is cooked in coconut milk. Imagine my surprise also when I tasted Nasi Lemak in Singapore – with fried sprats and other accompaniments! It gave me an insight into our shared culinary heritage. I try and make kiribath on the first of every month.

Milk Rice (Kiribath)

2 cups rice

Salt to taste

2 cups coconut milk

Cook the rice in four cups of water till very tender.

Add salt to taste. Pour in the coconut milk and allow most of it to be absorbed. Serve hot or cold with Seeni Sambol (page 50).

Serves 6

7 All Together Now

Eating out was a rarity when I was a child. We went to the occasional Chinese restaurant to celebrate a birthday or anniversary and happily ate Chopsuey. But sometimes on a shopping trip or if we went to visit my dad at the *Daily Mirror* – oh how I loved the rickety old lift and the vast rolls of paper that smelled so warm and toasty -- we would later stop for some shorteats at Green Cabin.

This café-cum-restaurant with its smell of frying cutlets in the air was a real treat for a hungry school-goer. It wasn't a fancy place, but even the short eats were served with cutlery. This is where my father taught us to use our forks and knives. And we poured tomato sauce onto everything.

Another speciality at Green Cabin was the lamprais, which was sold in banana leaf parcels. I learned that this meal-in-one of flavoured rice, topped with condiments, curries and sambols had Dutch origins. I haven't quite figured out how, save for the frikkadel which is part of the toppings.

If you make lamprais at home it's a fair amount of work. But once you have all the curries and relishes ready, it's just a matter of making up the parcels and baking them at lunch or dinner time. These are perfect for entertaining a large group.

Lamprais

For the Rice

2 cups jeera rice or samba if you can find it	2 inches pandanus leaf
	1 inch ginger, chopped
2 tbsp oil	4 cups warm light stock
1 onion, sliced	Salt to taste

Wash and drain the rice. Heat the oil in a cooker, put in the onion, the pandan leaf and ginger and sauté till the onion begins to change colour. Add the rice, stir about till the grains are all coated with the oil, pour in the warm stock and pressure-cook for ten minutes.

For the Meat Curry

- 400 gm, mutton, beef or chicken
- 1 tbsp oil
- 1 inch cinnamon
- 1 small onion, chopped
- 1 tsp ginger-garlic paste
- 1 tbsp Curry Powder (page 47)

Clean and chop the meat into small pieces. Heat the oil; add the cinnamon, onion and ginger-garlic paste. Sauté till done.

Add the meat and sauté till the colour of the meat changes to brown. Add the curry powder and about half a cup of water. Cook till the meat is done.

For the Unripe Banana Curry

- 1 unripe banana, cut into fingers
- Salt to taste
- A pinch of turmeric powder
- 1 tablespoon oil + for deep-frying
- 1 small onion, finely sliced
- 2 garlic cloves, chopped
- Small sprig curry leaves
- A pinch of chilli powder
- ½ cup coconut milk

Rub the banana pieces with salt and turmeric powder. Heat sufficient oil and deep-fry till pale golden. Set aside.

Heat 1 tablespoon oil; add the onion and the garlic and sauté till the onion begins to change colour. Add the curry leaves and the chilli powder.

Add the coconut milk; bring to the boil and then slip in the fried banana pieces. Let it simmer for five minutes.

For the Brinjal Pahi

- 1 medium purple brinjal
- ½ tsp salt
- A pinch of turmeric powder
- 1 tbsp oil
- ½ tsp mustard seeds
- ½ tsp red chilli powder
- ½ tsp fennel seeds
- A pinch of sugar
- 1 tsp vinegar

Cut the brinjal into thin strips, rub with salt and turmeric, drizzle with oil and grill in hot oven for about 10 minutes. The pieces should be golden brown. Set aside.

Grind the rest of the ingredients with vinegar. Place the brinjal in a pan, strain the mustard paste over it and simmer for five to ten minutes.

For the Frikkadels

200 gm minced chicken/lamb
2 tbsp breadcrumbs
Salt to taste
Pepper to taste
1 egg, beaten
1 tbsp chopped coriander
Oil for deep-frying

Mix all the ingredients together except the oil; form into small balls and deep-fry until deep brown.

To Assemble the Lamprais

6 large banana leaves
½ cup thick coconut milk

Wash and wipe dry the banana leaves. Hold over a flame till wilted. This prevents them from tearing.

Spread the leaves out, put a portion of rice at the centre of each.

Top with the a few tablespoons of each curry. Place two frikkadels on each mound. Pour a couple of tablespoons of coconut milk over the rice and curries.

Fold the leaves to form neat parcels and secure with toothpicks. Bake at 170°C/325°F/Gas Mark 3 for 30 minutes.

Serve the parcels. The rice is to be eaten straight from the banana leaves.

Makes 6 lamprais packets

8 Devilishly Good

My dad's elder brother who also lived in Colombo was simply Unca to me. He told the funniest jokes and whistled all manner of old tunes. It was a delight to listen to him and my dad reminisce about their days as children on a tea estate in Hatton. They had funny names for many of their relatives and Unca's fave story was about the man whose name was Selvam T V Sokkalingam Senthirumal Semmalpooban Pillaivaal Avargal. I'm not joking, Unca would say, with his wheezy laugh. And you mustn't forget the Avargal.

While it was my aunt who spent more time with us, Unca would occasionally suggest an outing. It was, invariably, to the beach in Mt Lavinia. And off we'd go my cousin and I. It was around that time a beachside resort called the Copa Cabana came up. These were wooden cottages on stilts and stood facing the sea. It was my first notion of a back-to-nature luxury experience. We never stayed in these, of course, but our beach outing was rounded off with a bite at La Langousterie, the seafront restaurant of this resort. And they served the most amazing devilled prawns. Devilled is Sri Lankan for chicken, fish, pork or beef with capsicums, tomato sauce and a diabolical bite. When I have over foodies who love their food really spicy, I make these devilled prawns, remembering Unca, who passed away not so long ago.

Devilled Prawns

- 2 tbsp oil
- 500 gm prawns, peeled and deveined
- 100 gm slender, green capsicums
- 1 large onion, cut into big wedges
- 1 tsp soya sauce
- 1 tsp Worcestershire sauce
- 1 tbsp tomato sauce
- ½ tsp black pepper powder
- Salt to taste

Heat the oil in a thick-bottomed pan; add the prawns, stir for a bit and then add the capsicums and onion. Add all the sauces and pepper powder, check for seasoning and add the salt if required, since the sauces contain salt. Let the peppers and onions keep their crunch. Serve as nibbles at a heavy drinking session.

Serves 4 as a snack

9 Something Fishy

We ate fish almost every day when we were children. It was a time when three proper meals, plus an evening snack, were made at home every day.

Restaurant visits were rare, and mainly celebratory. You didn't go to a restaurant because someone didn't feel like cooking at home.

And almost always for lunch we ate fish, rice and vegetables. I didn't much care for fish curry when I was a child, but really loved fried fish.

Some days it would be seer. On others, when budgets were slimmer, it would be small fish, such as silver fish, mackerel or sardines. I've never quite understood why these wonderful tasting fish are low down on the fishy social circuit.

And just as well for you can eat a whole plate of fried sardines without spending all that much.

There is nothing better than a pile of these fish, marinated in salt, lime juice and chilli powder fried to a crisp to be eaten up, bones and all. Of course, they give off such a strong smell all your neighbours will know you are eating sardines, too. But just because it's a humble fish, doesn't mean it has to be inelegant.

So, I've come up with this recipe which is perfectly good for the lunch table even when you're having company. It's vaguely inspired by a recipe I once saw in the Moro cookbook.

Fried and Stuffed Sardines

10 large sardines, gutted, scaled and washed

Juice of 1 lime

Salt to taste

Freshly ground pepper, as required

A small bunch parsley, washed and drained

1 small ripe red chilli

2-3 garlic cloves

2-3 cherry tomatoes

1 tbsp olive oil

Oil for shallow-frying

Pat dry the sardines and make a few diagonal slits on both sides of the fish. Marinate in half of the lime juice, salt and ground pepper.

Meanwhile, chop the parsley fine; mince the red chilli and garlic. Also chop the tomatoes. Mix everything together with remaining lemon juice and salt. Add the olive oil and mix. Set aside.

Shallow-fry the fish in a hot pan. Remove from the pan and stuff as much of the herb filling into the slits as they will hold.

Serve hot with crusty bread, aioli and a salad. Alternatively, drizzle the fish with some oil and grill in a hot oven.

Serves 2-3

How to Fry Fish without it Sticking

Most people find frying fish tricky because it tends to stick to the pan. This is caused by nothing more serious than impatience. Let the oil heat up well and let the fish fry for five minutes, depending on the type of fish and thickness, before you are tempted to turn it over.

Once the fish is well fried, the chances of it sticking are greatly reduced. It's when you try to lift out undercooked fish that it sticks. There's a scientific reason for this. Be patient and solve the problem.

10 For the Festive Table

This dish takes me back to all the festive meals of my childhood. For whenever there was a special lunch or dinner in Colombo, at the centre of the meal would be a vast platter piled high with pearly samba rice, tinted the most delicate yellow, and studded with cinnamon sticks, whole black peppercorns, cardamoms and cloves.

It was eaten with a line-up of Sri Lankan curries, vegetables and sambols. The dining table would literally groan under the weight of it all in many homes on occasions that called for yellow rice. It's like a pile of sunshine at the centre of the table, imbued with all the spices of this tropical island.

Yellow Rice (Kahabath)

2 cups samba rice, if you can get it, or jeera rice
2 tbsp ghee or oil
½ tsp peppercorns
6 cardamom pods
2 inches cinnamon
½ tsp cloves
2 inches pandanus leaf, if you can get your hands on it
1 large onion, finely sliced
1 inch ginger, chopped
A pinch of turmeric powder
4 cups thin coconut milk
Salt to taste

Wash and soak the rice for about an hour. Drain and set aside.

Heat the oil or ghee in a pressure cooker. Add the whole spices, the pandanus leaf and the onion and ginger. Sauté till the onion turns translucent.

Add the rice and stir-fry for 3-4 minutes. Add the turmeric powder and pour in the coconut milk. Add salt to taste. Close the cooker with the lid and pressure-cook for about 10 minutes.

Release the pressure, fluff up the rice and serve with a spicy chicken curry and salads.

Serves 6

11 Stuffed with Coconut

In a country like Sri Lanka, with its palm-fringed coast, there's no getting away from an abundance of coconut in your food. Many of the snacks and short-eats like cutlets and patties and kokis (known as rose cookies in Goa and Kerala) used to be deep-fried in coconut oil and no one raised any cholesterol scares.

Also, a lot of Sinhala cooking involves slow-cooking fish and vegetables in coconut milk scented with condiments and herbs and they are delightful! Grated coconut goes into all manner of dishes and relishes, such as the homely pol sambol which is merely fresh coconut pounded with red chillies, salt, shallots and lemon juice.

But one of my fave things to do with fresh coconut is to turn it into a sweet snack. Coconut pancakes are a Sri Lankan speciality and a great teatime treat. I use good jaggery whenever I have some at hand, but sugar will do just as well.

Coconut Pancakes

1 cup refined flour
2 cups milk
1 egg
A pinch of salt

1 cup grated coconut
½ cup good jaggery such as patali gur or sugar
A pinch of powdered cardamom

Whisk the flour with the milk, egg and salt to get a fairly thin, lump-free batter. Set aside. For the filling, melt the sugar or jaggery over a low heat, with a mere splash of water. Add the grated coconut and stir till it holds together. Add the cardamom and mix well.

Heat a griddle and make the pancakes. Pour in a ladleful of batter and spread gently to make a thin pancake. Once the surface is cooked turn over briefly. Remove the pancake from the griddle and lay it flat on a plate. Shape the coconut filling into cylindrical shape and place at one end of the pancake. Roll up tightly. Make all the pancakes this way. Eat warm or cool.

Makes about 8 rolls

How to Store Grated Coconut

If you've taken the trouble to break and grate a fresh coconut, store it well. Refrigerate in an uncovered container. It lasts longer this way. If you have stored coconut without grating, in the shell, you can revive it by soaking it for 30 minutes in cold water. Now grate and proceed.

To make milk from grated coconut that has been stored in the fridge, steep in hot water for about 10 minutes and then whizz in a blender and strain. Repeat a couple of times to extract all the milk.

12 Pasta for Comfort

My first notion of pasta was only macaroni cheese. It was made by Tonie Aunty, who taught me to read and introduced me to the joys of Winnie-the-Pooh, Amelia Jane and Toad of Toad Hall.

She was happier reading to us while we curled up on the couch – my cousin still owns it – than cooking, but what she made was exotica to me, different from the rice and curry meals, lovely as they were, in my own home.

Aunty served us pancakes with lime juice and sugar for breakast (la crepe citron-sucre, I later learned) and banana fritters with treacle for dessert.

When she was inclined to serve something slightly more complicated, she made Sinhala-style chicken curry with a dark home-made spice mixture.

This delectable main dish would accompany yellow rice and there would be sweet-hot pineapple curry, scented with cinnamon on the side. I adored the special meals at Aunty Tonie's place, for birthdays, anniversaries and, especially, Christmas.

But I also enjoyed the little treats she bought or whipped up when I went to spend weekends with my cousin. We would eat, perhaps packets of lamprais for lunch, brought from Green Cabin which had a huge reputation for this combination of rice, curries and relishes, with its Dutch origins.

For `tiffin' there would be a big slice of love cake or prawn puffs from Pereira and Sons, the popular Colombo bakers. Later we would amble down the charming lanes of Mt Lavinia, cross the railway line and hit the beach.

This was no sexed up shore, where foreign tourists sunned themselves in hired deck chairs. This was a local beach, the place where the local population gathered for an evening of none too expensive recreation. You could fly kites, build sand castles, eat boiled channa or vada, wade in the surf or simply sit on the golden sand and watch the sun go down.

As dusk fell, we would meander back home where more joys awaited. Aunty would read aloud from some fascinating adventure or teach us a poem. Dinner time and she would opt for something snappy and cheerful. It was in her home that I first ate macaroni.

It was very simple, tossed in butter with some processed grated cheese stirred in. The best kind of comfort food, before we settled down to bed time and ghost stories in the dark.

When, later, I ate out in fine restaurants, as a food critic and passionate foodie, I discovered the gems of Italian cooking and great pasta – from naughty puttanesca with its anchovy and caper bite, to elaborate crabmeat-stuffed ravioli and an unforgettable seafood chittara in PortoVenere on the Italian Riviera.

But there is a time for a simple, hit-the-spot pasta and Tagliatelle in cream sauce fits the bill. You cannot go wrong with this one and do not count calories while eating.

Pasta in Cream Sauce

250 gm pasta
Salt to taste
¾ cup thin cream
2 tbsp tasty cheese, grated
A tbsp of fresh herbs, such as dill
Pepper to taste

Bring a large pot of water to boil. Add a teaspoon of salt. When the water is at a rapid boil put in the pasta. Most pasta take about 12-13 minutes to cook.

Drain in a colander, but do not rinse in cold water.

To make the sauce, bring the cream to a gentle simmer over low heat. Put in the cheese, herbs you are using, salt and pepper.

Quickly toss in the pasta, stir well and serve hot. You could perk up this basic cream sauce by adding sautéed mushrooms, peeled, seeded and diced tomatoes or perhaps some crumbled bacon or bits of ham.

To make a sun-dried tomato cream sauce, soak sun-dried tomatoes in warm water for half an hour. Process in a blender till you have a red paste, stir this into the heated cream and then add your pasta.

Serves 2

How to Cook Pasta

Always use a large, voluminous pan and plenty of water for the pasta to move about in as it boils. Salt the water.

Drain the pasta when done, but do not rinse in cold water. Save some of the pasta cooking water to thin out your sauce if required.

13 Never Goes Out of Style

Right opposite my school, Methodist College in Colombo, was Pereira and Sons, the famous Colombo bakers. There it stood, tempting, beckoning with its piles of rock buns, flaky puffs, date cakes, chocolate rolls and the most delectable cream puffs. And it was out of bounds. Not all students were allowed to cross the road and go to Pereiras.

That was a privilege only accorded to prefects and senior students on the school committee. The only exception was on sports day when we could go, accompanied by a senior student, and buy what we liked before we took off to the sack races and the march past.

I would wait for the day, counting my hoard of pocket money. My sister always bought `matches' which were puff pastry sheets sandwiched with butter cream and jam. I always bought chocolate éclairs. They were and are my brother's favourite, too.

When I visit him in Oslo, I always find the time to bake a batch. The rich cream there and a topping of melted Freia chocolate make them extra special. But you can make very good éclairs or profiteroles as the French like to call them, too.

Chocolate Éclairs

60 gm flour	50 gm butter + for greasing
A pinch of salt	2 eggs

Sift the flour with the salt. Place 150 ml of water in a large pan; cut the butter into small pieces and add to the water. Bring to the boil.

When the butter melts, add the flour and stir vigorously till it thickens, pulls away from the sides and forms a ball. Remove from the heat and while still hot, beat the eggs into the flour mixture. This is best done with an electric mixer.

Prepare a baking tray by first greasing it lightly. Then rinse under a cold tap and shake off excess water. This is to have a moist base which will create steam and help your choux pastry rise well.

With a damp spoon form small buns or long tubes on the baking sheet. Bake at 200°C/400°F/Gas Mark 6 for 10 minutes, then increase the heat to 220°C/425°F/Gas Mark 7 and bake for a further ten minutes.

Once done, split and allow the steam to escape. If still moist return to a warm oven to dry out. The éclairs are now ready to be filled and served.

Fill the éclairs with whipped cream into which some icing sugar has been beaten. Or use butter cream. Top with melted chocolate or a chocolate glacé icing. For this, stir 4 tablespoons of icing sugar and 1 tablespoon sugar with 1 tablespoon hot water.

Choux pastry can also be used to make lovely savoury snacks. Flavour the dough with cheese and herbs and bake to make gougères. You can also split these and fill with a savoury mix of creamed salmon or chicken.

Makes about 12 éclairs

14 Roll it Up

There's no story or anecdote attached to this recipe. It's simply something I remembered during a conversation with a friend who had just returned from Colombo and was raving about the `short eats' which are the in-between snacks the city is justly famous for. Invariably, these are spicy mouthfuls, stuffed with fish, meat or potatoes, highly seasoned, as is the style with Sri Lankan food.

Chinese rolls – and I have no idea why they are thus named, save for some vague similarity with spring rolls – are a favourite snack in the bakeries and little food shops in Colombo. You may find something quite akin to these in Goa, where they are called pan rolls.

In Sri Lanka it's almost always tinned fish, such as mackerel which goes into these rolls. For some reason, it's called salmon; perhaps a throwback to the time when this luxury fish came canned. But what makes the filling delightful is all the spicing that goes into it.

It's blended with mashed potato to hold it together and has lots of onions, green chillies and pepper in it. The filling is wrapped in a pancake, which is then dipped in egg wash, crumbed and fried. Serve it as a teatime snack, or as a light supper with a salad such as coleslaw. You can also slice the rolls into one-inch pieces and serve them as finger foods with drinks. Here's the recipe:

Chinese Rolls

For the Filling

1 tin (400 gm) mackerel in brine or oil

300 gm potatoes, boiled, peeled and mashed roughly

2 tbsp oil

1 large onion, finely chopped

1 tsp grated ginger

2 green chillies, chopped

½ tsp chilli powder

½ tsp black pepper powder

Salt to taste

1 tsp lime juice

200 gm breadcrumbs

Oil for deep-frying

For the Pancakes

1 cup refined flour

A pinch of salt

2 eggs

1 cup milk

For the filling, drain the fish and flake it by breaking down with a fork. Set aside.

Heat 2 tablespoons oil and add the onions, ginger and green chillies. Fry till onions are translucent. Put in the chilli powder and pepper powder; sauté for a couple of minutes.

Add the fish and the potatoes. Stir everything together, till the mixture holds together. Add salt to taste and the lime juice. Mix and set aside.

For the pancakes, beat together flour, salt and eggs. Gradually add the milk. to get a thin batter of pouring consistency, free of lumps. Add more water if required. Now pour on a hot griddle or tawa, to make a thin pancake about 6-inch in diameter.

Do not overcook. Lift off and lay flat on a plate. Place some filling down the middle of the pancake. Tuck in the two ends of the pancake and roll up. You should have a well-sealed roll. Make as many rolls possible with the remaining filling, working quickly.

Now dip each roll in the left over batter and roll in breadcrumbs. Heat the oil and deep-fry, a few at a time, until golden brown. You can make up the rolls and store them in advance before frying.

You can use cooked minced meat or a mixture of vegetables instead of the fish. And there you have it - an old-fashioned snack that hits the spot every time.

Makes about 18 rolls

Make Your Own Breadcrumbs

Save up the end slices of your bread in the fridge. When you have collected about 20 slices, toast them in a moderate oven till crisp. Cool and powder in the blender. Store in an airtight container for cutlets.

15 The Spice Inside

I do go on about the short eat shops in Colombo, don't I? But they are stocked with such delights, especially if you like the spicy kick of things. There are the small bites, like cutlets and patties, and then the substantial items like maalu paan – which means fish bread. It's simply a bread roll stuffed with spiced tinned fish and potato and lots of spice. They made a fab after-school snack. And my tuckshop had seeni sambol buns, which were good, too.

I bake these bread rolls whenever I need an easy-to-carry snack. They are also good for when you want a light supper. It's important that you get good quality yeast, so your buns will rise nicely and also taste good. Otherwise, there isn't very much to this dish.

Stuffed Buns

2 cups refined flour
2 tsp instant dried yeast
A pinch of sugar
Salt to taste

For the Filling

Chinese Rolls (page 35)
Oil for greasing
1 egg, beaten (optional)

Ensure your mixing bowl is warm. Put in the flour, mix in the instant yeast, sugar and salt.

Add 200 ml lukewarm water gradually (you may not need all of it) and knead well for about ten minutes till you have a soft, smooth dough.

Cover with a damp cloth and leave to rise for about an hour. Then, punch the dough down and form into golf ball-sized balls. Make a hollow in the centre of each ball and put in a tablespoon of the filling. Close to seal and place on an greased baking sheet. Leave to rise again, for about 10 minutes.

Bake at 200°C/400°F/Gas Mark for about 20 minutes until well risen and brown. Brush with beaten egg and return to the oven briefly if you want a glossy top.

Makes about 8 buns

16 Steamy Affair

Puttu is, of course, a Kerala breakfast special, frequently paired with kadala curry. This crumbly, steamed dish is made from red or white rice flour. In Sri Lanka it's sometimes done a little differently, made with refined flour which has been roasted till fragrant and a very pale brown.

Then it's moistened with water, aerated by mixing ever so lightly with the fingertips and then steamed in a tube. Nowadays it's a stainless contraption which sits on top of your pressure cooker lid. But I remember a time when the puttu was steamed in my home in a bamboo. The base would be wrapped in cloth to sit snugly on top of a vessel of boiling water.

At the bottom of the bamboo was a disc carved from coconut shell with a few holes in it to let the steam through. Talk about eco-friendly cooking utensils!

If you do not have a puttu steamer, you can place the puttu on a cloth lining a steamer and cook it that way, too. But it will be far less attractive. My sister is the best puttu maker I know. And she does it in minutes. I use my own technique to get it right. Read all about it.

Puttu

2 cups refined flour

A pinch of salt

2 tbsp grated coconut

Put the refined flour in a thick-bottomed karhai and roast over low heat.

Stir constantly till the flour emits a toasty aroma and changes colour to a pale brown. This takes time and patience and cannot be rushed. It will take about 30 minutes.

When cool, sift to remove lumps. Place in a wide bowl; add the salt and sprinkle 100 ml hot water. Experienced cooks can just rub the flour and water together and make delicate granules.

What I do is to sprinkle a little water and then mix with my hand whisk. Keep adding water and mixing gently with the whisk till there is no dry flour left. It should all turn into small granules.

To steam, put some water in a pressure cooker, cover. Put the disc with the holes in it into the puttu tube, scatter in a little coconut and then put in the puttu gently.

Fill up to the top and then place the tube on the vent of the cooker lid. When the steam begins to release from the top, cover the tube. Cook for 3 minutes and push the puttu out. It should fall in fat, soft lengths. Serve with coconut milk or Sodhi (page 57).

If you do not have a puttu steamer, line a steamer with a damp cloth, place the flour on it and steam for about 8 minutes.

Serves 2

17 Something Aussie

For a long time no one really thought of Australia as a place of fine food. Today though it's definitely a gourmet destination – expert chefs drawing from the country's melting pot nature come up with dishes that fuse all manner of ethnic ingredients with exciting cooking styles. But when I was a young exchange student in Brisbane in the early '80s, that wasn't the case. It was pretty much meat-and-potatoes eating in most places.

My host mother, Barney Moore, was a warm, wonderful soul, but a reluctant cook. It came as a shock then to see dinner – or tea as it's known there – being prepared. None of the chopping, roasting, pounding, frying that went into my mother's meals here. Barney would simply rouse herself from whatever soap she was watching on TV, go to the cavernous deep freezer, pick out the steaks and plonk them in the electric skillet. If she felt like it, she made mashed potatoes from an instant pack.

Else, it would be stewed tomatoes from a can. But the meat was of top quality and I came to enjoy these basic Aussie teas, day after day. Still, it was a welcome change to find myself heading for the bush to spend a winter break. 'Chinchilla', a T-shirt I bought said, 'Just east of too far west'.

There, in the Wolskis' rambling ranch, surrounded by gum trees in which koala bears huddled, I had my taste of the Aussie outback. While in my Brisbane home we almost always ate Weetbix and cold milk for brekker, here it was a mammoth hot meal of homemade sausages and eggs and gravy. That, too, almost at daybreak, before the men in the family headed off to their various tasks on the farm.

One day, Mrs Wolski made mountains of corned beef sandwiches with home-cured meat and we went to the local fete – with a rodeo show. All the farm ladies brought baked goodies to feed the crowd.

I'll always remember the lamingtons from there and from other fetes in Australia. At slightly more upscale gatherings it would be the pavlova – that concoction of meringue and cream – but the lamingtons are really as easy as pie! So here goes.

Lamingtons

1 recipe Butter Cake (page 12)
300 gm icing sugar, sifted
50 gm cocoa powder, sifted
200 gm desiccated coconut

Cut the cake into neat two-inch squares. Set aside.

Gently heat the icing sugar, cocoa and half a cup of water over low heat till you have an icing of pouring consistency.

Spread the coconut on a large square sheet of paper. Using either a skewer or fork, dip the pieces of cake in the icing and roll in the coconut.

Work quickly as the icing tends to harden and you won't get the finish you want.

Makes about 20 squares

18 DIY Pizza

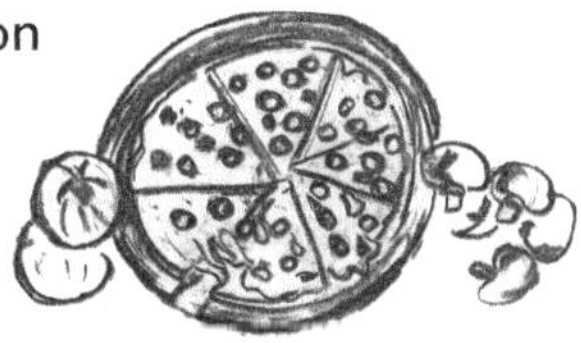

I remember my first pizza. It was in Australia, on the Gold Coast, to be precise. My Aussie host family had taken me there on a weekend trip to show me possibly the country's top tourist attraction after the Opera House, the Sydney Harbour bridge and the Great Barrier Reef.

I had never seen so many blonde, tanned, bathing beauties in the scantiest bikinis in one place. Being no beach babe myself and after a couple of disastrous attempts at surf-boarding I looked to the other pleasures on this famous strip of sand. There was always the food. We were on a caravan holiday and ate cheap for the most part. But coming from Sri Lanka, still untouched by the American fastfood chain invasion, I was fascinated by hamburgers, malted milks and fries. Imagine my wonderment then, when we entered a pizza parlour.

It wasn't quite assembly line food, for the pizzas were freshly tossed and baked on order. The cooks did a bit of showing off while tossing the pizza and I distinctly remember one dough base sticking to the ceiling, as a result of some over-enthusiastic pizza tossing, I surmised. Customers chose the toppings from a line-up of containers. It was mostly American-style stuff – canned pineapple chunks, corn and cubes of ham. I think I loved the idea of the pizza more than the way it really tasted. But it was the beginning of a fascination for what a piece of dough, some tomato sauce, cheese and a bit of imagination could amount to.

My culinary travels have taken me far from the Hawaiian pizza of the Gold Coast to eat a superlative pizza margarita in Florence, under the shadow of the magnificent cathedral, and some top class pizzas right here in Bangalore. Chef Manu Chandra of Olive Beach bakes a super version and I like mine scattered with arugula and the thinnest slivers of prosciutto. To tell you the truth, though, I'm no pizza person. But I do love baking them.

There is such satisfaction in turning out a pizza that looks utterly professional and you know costs less than a third of what the pizza chains charge for their mediocre fare. Try this in your kitchen. All you need is the recipe, a good kneading hand and someone to say 'Wow, you did that at home?'

Pizza Margarita

For the Pizza Base

2 cups refined flour
1 tbsp instant yeast
½tsp salt
3 tbsp olive oil

For the Tomato Sauce

500 gm ripe tomatoes
1 tbsp olive oil
3-4 garlic cloves, finely chopped
Salt to taste

For the Topping

1 cup grated mozzarella
A handful of basil leaves, washed and torn

To make the pizza base, stir the yeast and salt through the flour in a large bowl. Pour in the olive oil and add 200 ml lukewarm water gradually to make a soft, sticky dough.

Knead for 10 minutes. Form into a ball, cover with a damp cloth and set aside for an hour.

To make the sauce, peel the tomatoes. Chop roughly, removing any hard or semi-ripe centres. You can also rub the tomato against the coarse side of a grater. Catch the juice and pulp in a large bowl. You will be left with the peel which can be thrown away.

Heat the oil in a thick-bottomed pan and add the garlic. Ensure that the heat is moderate and the garlic does not burn. As the garlic releases its tantalising aroma, empty the tomatoes into the oil. Add the salt and bring to a brisk boil; reduce the heat and allow to simmer till the sauce thickens. You can stir in a few torn basil leaves as the sauce cools.

To make the pizza, preheat the oven to 220°C/425°F/Gas Mark 7, while you assemble the pizza. Take a baking tray and rub some oil over the surface.

Divide the risen dough into two parts. Take one part and pat into a circle on the tray, making it as thin as possible, without leaving any holes.

Prick the surface with a fork and then spread some of the tomato sauce over it. Be sparing with the sauce, you don't want to make the base soggy.

Sprinkle the grated cheese on top and pop into the oven. You can use the cheese in thin slices if you wish. If your oven is well heated, the pizza will be ready in about 10 minutes. It should have a thin, crisp base and the cheese bubbling away.

Makes 2 large pizzas

How to Peel Tomatoes

Most recipes that call for peeled tomatoes will ask you to blanch the tomatoes and then pull off the skins. I have a simpler method: take a really ripe tomato and run the blunt edge of a knife from top to bottom over the tomato. Then run the knife in the opposite direction. It will now be quite easy to slice off the top of the tomato and pull off the skin with the help of a knife.

19 Movie Time, But No Popcorn

Madurai is now my `native place', that peculiar term by which we pinpoint where our roots lie. When my family moved there it was a culture shock to me: the fact that it could be a town and still so bucolic in every sense.

Life revolved around the awe-inspiring temple of the Fish-Eyed Goddess and all the activity around it. You can pray, listen to classical music performances in the magical dusk when the scent of jasmine rents the air and, of course, shop in the quaint nooks around this most wonderful of edifices.

You can shop here for everything from bangles, to footwear and have your saree blouses stitched up even as you wait. Still, if you want a bit more `action', there's no looking beyond the cinema halls. In movie-crazy Tamil Nadu, Madurai manages to be a flag-bearer. And I must admit I'm something of a movie fiend myself. I spent all the weeks of all the years I spent in Madurai watching films. I've seen all the Kamal Haasan and Rajnikanth films that released during that time. And also the romantic films of Mohan (does anyone remember that everyday hero?), and some of the path-breaking stuff that K Balachander offered up in that period. I saw a minimum of three films a week. We went, dressed in our half-sarees, flowers in our hair and a little extra money to eat something during the intermission. Not caramel popcorn and Pepsi.

This was far more exciting stuff. There were really nice murukku, very spicy samosa, held within a crisp envelope and, my favourite muttai or egg bajji. It's simplest of things – just hardboiled eggs dipped in a spicy gram flour batter and deep-fried to a spongy-crispy texture. It's totally without pretension and I enjoy it.

Of course, calorie-conscious as one is, you don't often eat this kind of thing these days. But when I take my niece to the movies in Madurai these days, we still have a muttai bajji wrapped in a square of newspaper.

Here is how you can do it at home:

Muttai Bajji

4 hardboiled eggs
1 cup gram flour
½ tsp salt
A pinch of chilli powder
A pinch of garam masala
A pinch of soda bicarbonate
Oil for deep-frying

Mix the gram flour with the salt, spices and soda bicarbonate. Add half a cup of water to make a thick batter.

Quarter the hardboiled eggs, dip each quarter into the batter and deep-fry in the hot oil. Drain on absorbent paper and serve hot. Munch while you watch your fave flick on DVD.

Makes 16 bajji

For Perfect Hardboiled Eggs

Place the eggs in a single layer in a pan with cold water. Bring to a rapid boil and allow to cook for 4-5 minutes.

Take off the heat, cover and leave for 15 minutes. Now, peel under cold water and proceed.

20 You Can Make Appam, Too

When I go home to Madurai these days I drive down. But there was a time when the Tuticorin Express was my preferred mode of transport. It was most convenient. I would have dinner with a friend and board the train at nine-thirty or so.

For ten hours, absolved of all responsibility and tucked into my a/c berth I was free to listen to music or read by the dim lights. At half past six the train would reach Kodai road and I could see the mist-wrapped Kodai hills in the distance. Time for a kaapi.

An hour later, the train would pull into Madurai junction, one of the south's best kept stations, and in less than half an hour I would be home for breakfast.

Almost always it would be appam, my mother's super-speciality version, that was served up for breakfast. It was a lot of work, involving soaking the rice, grinding it, sieving, then mixing in with coconut milk and yeast and leaving it to ferment.

But she would make it all seem effortless. And then dozens of hot appam with their lacy crisp edges and satin pillow centres would emerge to be gobbled down with sambol.

I would not consider myself an expert at appam making. But my sister has taken over from my mother and makes excellent appam with the same effortlessness. Here is my family recipe:

Appam

2 cups raw rice	A pinch of sugar
1 coconut	Salt to taste
A pinch of yeast	A pinch of soda bicarbonate

Wash and soak the rice for about three hours. Break the coconut and reserve the coconut water.

Dissolve the yeast in the coconut water with a pinch of sugar and set aside. Drain the rice.

Grind 2 tablespoons of rice to a coarse powder, the consistency like that of semolina.

Grate half a coconut and process in a blender with small amounts of water.

Squeeze out the coconut milk. Do this several times till you get about 3 cups of coconut milk. Grind the remaining rice to a fine paste, adding the coconut milk.

Pour the batter into a large vessel. Cook the coarsely ground rice in half a cup of water till you have a thick, clear kanji. Add it to the batter.

Pour in the coconut water and yeast mixture. Add the salt, mix well and leave to ferment for about 8 hours. Now you are ready to make the appam.

The batter should be thin and smooth, like pancake mix. Add the soda bicarbonate just before you start making the appam.

To make the apppam, you need a small karhai. A non-stick is useful if you do not have a well-seasoned pan.

Heat the karhai, grease lightly with a cloth dipped in oil. Pour in a large ladle of batter and give the karhai a slow turn.

The batter should coat the sides and run down to form a thick centre. Cover and cook for 2-3 minutes. You should have appam with a golden crust and a satiny pillow centre.

Lift out carefully and serve with Seeni Sambol (page 50), curries, butter, jam or anything else you fancy.

Makes about 20 appam

21 It's All in the Curry Powder

I have been trying to cut down my red meat consumption to bring some discipline into my eating habits. But there was one dish that always tested my resolve and broke it down: my mother's mutton curry. While I can count dozens of my mother's dishes which I loved as a child and continued to enjoy, this one probably gets in ahead of the rest. Whenever I visited home, my mother would always make it, if it wasn't a no-meat, religious occasion, that is.

The quality of the mutton in Madurai is superb, and we have been buying our meat from the same butcher for two decades now. I know other cooks who make a ceremony of cooking chicken or mutton. My mom did it effortlessly. That's because, at the heart of it is a perfect curry powder, which was always at hand. Once you've got that right, you simply cannot go wrong. Here, first, the curry powder recipe.

All-purpose Curry Powder

1 kg dried red chillies
500 gm coriander seeds
100 gm cumin seeds
100 gm peppercorns
50 gm aniseed
A handful of curry leaves dried in the sun
200 gm par-boiled rice, toasted until popping

Get all the ingredients together and have them machine-ground at a reliable grinding store.

Mutton Curry

1 kg, good quality mutton, cut into cubes
8 garlic cloves, peeled
1 inch ginger, peeled
4 tbsp grated coconut
2 tbsp oil
200 gm shallots, peeled and roughly chopped
Sprig of curry leaves
4 tbsp curry powder
1 tbsp coriander seeds, roasted and powdered

Wash the mutton and set aside. Pound the garlic and ginger together to make a rough paste. Roast the coconut till golden brown and grind to a fine paste, adding a little water.

Heat the oil in a pressure cooker, add the shallots, ginger-garlic and curry leaves. Sauté till shallots begin to colour.

Add the curry powder and the meat. Stir well for a few minutes. Add a cup of water and pressure-cook for three whistles.

Cool; open the lid of the pressure cooker and add the ground coconut and coriander powder and bring to a boil. You should have a rich, brown gravy and tender meat.

Serve with rice.

Serves 6

22 Make Mine Curry

I am an adventurous eater. It's part of the job of a food critic. So, I will tackle most anything eagerly – from escargot in a cosy restaurant in Rheims to smelly snail soup in the Djemaa el fnaa in Marrakesh. I waded boldly into sashimi territory when I was first introduced to it and think it's okay to eat frog's legs. But give me a choice and I'd go rushing back to the familiar and the comforting.

So, while I, too, can extol the virtues of perfectly grilled John Dory or Chilean sea bass, when it comes to fish, nothing does it for me like a good homestyle fish curry, thick, red, spicy and a little tart. With the fish well done and steeped in the gravy's flavour. Give me such a curry and a plate of hot rice and I will ask for nothing more. It's great with paratha and roti, too, especially leftover and reheated the next day. Mackerel, sardines and seer fish are perfect for cooking this way.

Hot Fish Curry

500 gm fish
Salt to taste
1 tsp turmeric powder
Juice of ½ a lime
1 tbsp tamarind, soaked in a cup of water
3 tbsp Curry Powder (page 47)
2 tbsp oil
½ tsp mustard seeds
A pinch of fenugreek seeds
1 inch ginger, chopped
3-4 garlic cloves, chopped
200 gm shallots, chopped
A sprig of curry leaves
½ cup thick coconut milk

Clean and gut the fish. Seer should be cut in cubes. If using sardines, keep whole. Mackerels can be sliced into two each.

Rub the fish with a little salt, half a teaspoon of turmeric powder and the lime juice and set aside for 15 minutes. This takes the fishy odours away. Rinse and pat dry.

Now, extract the tamarind juice from the soaked pulp. Add to it the curry powder, the remaining turmeric powder, salt to taste and the fish. Let the fish remain in this mixture for an hour or so.

To make the curry, heat the oil in a thick-bottomed pan, throw in the mustard and fenugreek, ginger and garlic and the shallots. Add the curry leaves.

Sauté on low heat till the onions soften and begin to colour. Do this patiently, as it has a remarkable effect on the final taste. When the onions have softened and coloured without browning, pour in only the marinade and half a cup of water.

Bring to a steady boil; now slip in the fish. Let the fish cook and the gravy thicken. Pour in the coconut milk and simmer for a few minutes. Serve with plain rice or paratha.

Serves 4

23 A Sweet-hot Sambol

A seeni sambol, which means sugar sambol, is a popular Sri Lankan relish which accompanies meals of idiappam and hodhi. Onions are sliced into thin slivers, slow-fried in plenty of oil until they meld into a caramel goldenness and then seasoned with cinnamon, lots of chilli powder, sugar and Maldive fish. Some people add a little thick coconut milk as well.

My sister, a tomboy who never stepped foot in the kitchen in her growing up years, is now a fabulous cook. And superfast she is too. Whenever I travel to Madurai, she packs me a delightful meal for the return journey.

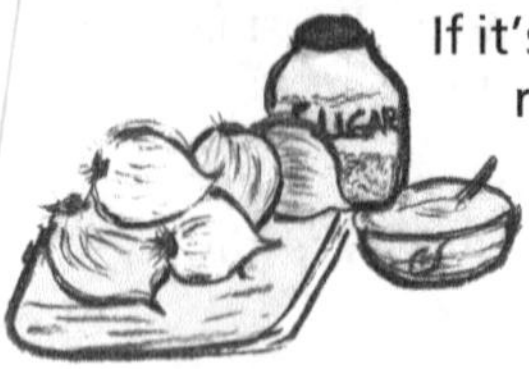

If it's breakfast or dinner she makes idiappam with red rice flour and the accompaniment is seeni sambol. Though she doesn't sweat over it too much, just throwing in everything together, it turns out just wonderful. Here is the quick way.

Seeni Sambol

500 gm onions
4 tbsp oil
Salt to taste
1 tbsp coarsely pounded chilli powder
2 sprigs curry leaves
2 tsp Maldive fish chips (optional)
1 tsp sugar

Peel and slice the onions fine. Heat the oil, put in the onions and sauté on low heat till the onions soften and the colour changes to light pink.

Add the salt, chilli powder, curry leaves and the Maldive fish chips, if using.

Cook on low heat, stirring frequently, until the onions begin to caramelise. Serve with Rotti (page 18), Appam (page 45) or idiappam. It's also a great sandwich filling.

Serves 4 as an accompaniment

24 Baking for the Man in My Life

Dev, my 12-year-old nephew is a regular little foodie. When he was much younger, if I was visiting my folks and if he caught the whiff of baking when he returned from school, he would walk in – still grubby from play – asking, 'is Periamms cooking?' A picky eater, he enjoys a few things: the dal I make, the French fries, the pizza... but most of all, my cakes and pastries.

He loves especially this simple cake, which is sweetened with honey and has almonds scattered over the top. It's not a kiddy cake, in the sense it's not overly sweet or creamy. It's more an adult cake for teatime. But Devu loves it. And when I visit, he almost always adds this to his request of things I should make. This one is dedicated for one of the best little men in my life:

Honey Cake

- 50 gm butter
- 25 gm caster sugar
- 125 gm honey
- 175 gm flour
- ½ tsp soda bicarbonate
- ½ tsp mixed spice of nutmeg, cinnamon and cloves
- 1 egg
- 2 tbsp milk
- 25 gm almonds, slivered
- 2 tbsp honey, to drizzle

Preheat the oven to 180°C/350°F/Gas Mark 4.

Grease and line an 8-inch cake tin. Heat the butter, sugar and honey together till just melted. Set aside. Beat the egg and milk and keep aside. Sift the flour, soda bicarbonate and spice powder into a large bowl. Make a well in the flour mixture and pour in the melted butter mixture.

Beat well to incorporate and then add the beaten egg and milk mixture. Mix and pour into the prepared cake tin. Sprinkle the slivered almonds on top and bake for 35 minutes or till a skewer inserted into the cake comes out clean. Drizzle with the honey. Slice and serve.

Cuts into 8 slices

25 The Goodness of Milk

Before I began my career as a journalist I spent a short while teaching Montessori in a somewhat upmarket school in Madurai. It was a deeply satisfying and rewarding experience. And if teachers got paid better I believe I may have continued in that line. Just to be able to spend hours in the company of all those beautiful little children was attractive enough a prospect.

The teachers also made a happy group. And our shared lunches were a time to not only exchange notes about the various children in our care, but also to trade recipes. Kausalya, the vice principal, a wise and efficient lady, was also a fab cook. It is she who taught me how to pack phulka that didn't turn dry and also paruppusili, which is a healthful, crumbly mixture of dal and a vegetable such as cluster beans. But best of all was the paal payasam she brought on special occasions. Here is the recipe for a traditional south Indian sweet to round off a festive meal. Do not be tempted to pressure cook. This is one recipe where patience pays off.

Paal Payasam

1 litre whole milk

3 tbsp rice, such as jeera or sona masuri

5 tbsp sugar

Wash the rice. Pour the milk into a thick-bottomed pan and put in the rice. Bring to the boil; reduce the heat and allow the milk to simmer to reduce in volume. Stir frequently. The rice will cook in the milk and turn mushy. Rub the grains along the sides of the pan to crush them.

The payasam is ready when the rice is cooked soft and the milk is reduced to about one-third its original volume. Remove from heat and add the sugar. Stir and serve warm or cold. You could add cardamoms, saffron, nuts or raisins, but I think this payasam is at its best when it's served without adornment.

Serves 4-5

26 Yes, They Eat Banana Stems

My mother, the ever-enthusiastic cook, would think nothing of attempting a dish that involved 14 ingredients and eight or ten steps. When it came to cooking, no effort was too much. But then she also had a penchant for making some very elementary dishes and they would turn out just superb.

This healthy pachadi is one such. It relies on nothing more than yogurt and the freshest insides of a banana stem. Freshness is key and I don't always find banana stem of this quality on the supermarket shelves here.

Whereas in Madurai a trip to the morning's uzhavar sandhai or farmer's market would yield some superb fresh produce and banana stems would be among the pickings at the stalls specialising only in banana leaves, stems, banana flowers and unripe green banana.

I do enjoy traipsing through this uzhavar sandhai every time I am in Madurai. It is such a treat to be able to see and buy vegetables and greens that have been plucked or harvested only hours before.

There are dozens of varieties of brinjals to be bought, to be simmered in a sambar or to be turned into puli kozhambu, butter beans which can make a great bean soup, yams and gourds and a wide range of greens.

All of which makes you want to think of ways to cook these wonderfully fresh vegetables. But, back to the banana stem pachadi.

Banana Stem Pachadi

8 inches banana stem	Salt to taste
1 cup fresh yogurt	A few curry leaves, hand torn

Peel away the tough outer layers of the banana stem to get the tender kernel.

Cut into thin discs; stacking a couple of discs at time and cut into matchstick size strips.

Drop these into acidulated water (water which has a squeeze of lime juice or a little yogurt in it). Beat the yogurt and add salt to taste. Remove the banana stem pieces from the water; squeeze and drop them into the yogurt.

Add the curry leaves. That's all it takes. It's full of health and very delicious served at any vegetarian meal. You can season the pachadi with a seasoning of mustard seeds and skinless split black gram, but it can do perfectly well without it.

Serves 6

27 Greens, Chettinad-style

My mother had a penchant for making friends and nurturing relationships over great distances and long spans of time. My parents lived in Madras for a short spell and during this time my mother befriended the neighbour of a friend.

Deivanai-amma is from Chettinad and embodies all the efficiencies and the cooking skills the women of this region are justly famous for. Once my parents moved back to Madurai, Deivanai-amma was a frequent visitor and my mother would make her prepare her specialities. Among these were citron pickles and molagapodi for idli which could be stored for future use.

She also made fabulous paniyaram, fluffy discs made of a sweet batter of rice and skinless split black gram. It was such a warm and wonderful feeling to see my mom and her, bustling about in the kitchen, chatting about their children, temples, religious fasts to observe --I never caught them gossiping about people – and cooking up the delights of Chettinad. From Deivanai-amma's repertoire I specially adore this simple dish of greens.

Keerai Masiyal

2 bunches (approx. 300 gm) greens, such as chowli	2 green chillies, slit
3 tbsp skinless split green gram	1 garlic clove
1 tbsp oil	2 tbsp coconut milk
6 shallots, chopped	Salt to taste
	2 tsp ghee

Clean and wash the greens (see below).

Drain and chop roughly. Wash the skinless split green gram. Heat the oil in a pressure cooker and put in the shallots. Sauté and add the greens, stir till wilted, put in the split green gram and about a cup of water and cook for five minutes (one whistle).

When the pressure releases completely, open the lid and mash the greens and dal till you have a thick purée. Crush the garlic clove and add to the purée.

Pour in the coconut milk. Add the salt and mix well. Add the ghee and serve hot with rice.

Serves 6

How to Wash Greens

The trick to washing greens is to use a vast quantity of water and lift the greens out rather than let the water drain through them. Take a large vessel and fill with water.

Put in the greens, move them about, rinse and lift out. Pour out the water and the grit, refill with water and repeat. Do this at least three times. Your greens will now be grit-free.

28 Snake Gourd, Sans the Boredom

This is my maternal grandmother's recipe. Like most of the women in my family she was an exceptionally good cook. A small eater, who shunned many things such as chicken, she would still make fabulous chicken curries and sukka.

And after a thunderstorm, she would pick wild mushrooms from the garden in her home in Gampola and turned it into a wonderful stir-fry with red chillies and fennel.

The dish that follows is an innovative way to use snake gourd. This is not a veggie that climbs very high on the glam charts, being, for most part, water.

But my grandmother's version which my mother used to make and us, after her, turns it into something special.

Snake Gourd with Egg

- 500 gm tender snake gourd
- 1 tbsp oil
- Salt to taste
- A pinch of turmeric powder
- ½ tsp chilli powder
- A few curry leaves
- 2 eggs

Scrape the snake gourd and rinse. Slice the snake gourd into thin slices as for onion rings.

Remove the white membrane and the seeds. Heat the oil in a frying pan and put in the snake gourd. Add the salt, turmeric powder and chilli powder and stir-fry till done.

Spread them out to make a single layer. Then break the eggs over the snake gourd slices.

Do not scramble. Once the eggs are set, lift out and serve with rice and curry or chapati.

Serves 4

29 A Coconut Milk Stew

Coastal restaurants here, which serve Kerala food, offer up the combination of appam and stew. Though I thoroughly enjoy these meals, I find the stews frequently a tad too dense and thickened by more than just coconut milk. The Sri Lankan version of this is a far thinner, fragrant concoction. Big chunks of potato are cooked in the second extract of coconut milk with shallots, green chillies, a stick of cinnamon, rampe or pandanus leaf and lemon grass. Tomatoes are added sometimes. Once everything has simmered away and the milk is infused with the scent of the herbs and spices, the thick extract of coconut milk is added and the hodhi or sodhi (as it's known in Tamil) is ready to serve. Interestingly, in Sri Lankan homes and restaurants, the hodhi is served with idiappam, Puttu (page 38) and even bread, but rarely with Appam (page 45) as is the practice here. I think it's especially good with homemade idiappam, soft, white and lacy, waiting to soak up the fragrant, creamy hodhi. Here is my version.

Sodhi or Kiri Hodhi

200 gm potatoes, boiled and peeled
2 cups thin coconut milk
1 medium onion, thinly sliced
1 medium tomato, chopped
2 green chillies, slit
2 inches fresh pandanus
1 inch cinnamon
½ tsp cumin seeds
A pinch of turmeric powder
Salt to taste
½ cup thick coconut milk
1 tsp lime juice

Cut the potatoes into large chunks and set aside. Place rest of the ingredients, except the thick coconut milk and lemon juice into a pan and bring to a boil. Reduce the heat and let it simmer for about 10 minutes till the milk is infused with the spices and herbs. Add the potatoes and the thick coconut milk.

Heat through and add the lemon juice. Serve with idiappam or Puttu (page 38). It's very good with warm, crusty bread, too.

Serves 2

30 A Different Sort of Egg Curry

This was the store cupboard meal in my house. We had it on days when we didn't have fish or meat. What it is, is an omelette in a typically Sri Lankan curry with coconut milk.

The texture of the omelette made it seem somewhat meaty and we loved having it with stringhoppers, bread, rice or even noodles, if you please. I make it frequently when I am pushed to cooking with what's in the store cupboard. It's excellent.

Omelette Curry

3 eggs, lightly beaten	1 onion, thinly sliced
Salt to taste	1 sprig curry leaves
A pinch of turmeric powder	2 ripe tomatoes, chopped
1 tablespoon oil	1 tablespoon Curry Powder (page 47)
1 inch ginger, chopped	
2 garlic cloves, chopped	1 cup coconut milk

Season the beaten eggs with salt and turmeric powder and make a thick omelette.

Allow to cool and cut into large squares. Set aside. Heat the oil in a pan; put in the ginger, garlic, onion and the curry leaves.

Sauté on low heat till the onion begins to change colour. Add the tomatoes; stir-fry till the tomatoes turn pulpy. Put in the curry powder and fry for a minute or two.

Now pour in the coconut milk and simmer. Turn off the heat and slip in the omelette squares. Serve hot.

Serves 2

31 Perfectly Pickled

My mother was a tireless cook. If there were six people at home and each had a different food preference she would happily, unstintingly satisfy every individual taste and craving.

I have never known her to actually cook something for herself, leave alone sit down and eat at leisure. In her view, there was always so much to be done, cooking three meals, packing lunches for the grandchildren, making snacks, masala powders, carrying lunches for her pregnant friends and so on. Plus, she kept a spotless home.

When this dynamic, active woman fell ill, terminally, we heard, our world crashed around us and the buzz in my mother's kitchen slowly fizzled out. Her loss of appetite was one of the worst aspects of the illness. We tried feeding her all the things she might like, realising she had never really expressed a great desire for anything, except the odd piece of seer fish or a slice of home-baked cake. That's when she asked for some achcharu to be made. This is the Sri Lankan pickle which can really perk up meals.

There always used to be huge bottles of this pickle in my home. The making of the season's achcharu was quite an event. Jocelyn, an old cook, would be summoned on these occasions. She was also the one brought in for making konde kavum the rice flour and treacle oil cakes - and jack seed curry in a black masala. This achcharu gets better with keeping.

Sri Lankan Achcharu

500 gm shallots, peeled

100 gm fresh, green chillies with stalks

200 gm carrots, peeled and cut into fingers

1 small unripe green papaya, peeled, seeded and cut into fingers

100 gm tender French beans, cut into fingers

50 gm mustard seeds

Salt to taste

A pinch of turmeric powder

1 tsp red chilli powder

150 ml white vinegar

2 tbsp sugar

Wash the shallots and pat dry. Wash and pat dry the chillies, make a small slit in each. The vegetables should all be dried well and moisture-free.

Grind the mustard seeds, salt, turmeric and chilli powder to a fine paste, using a tablespoonful of the vinegar. Set aside. Poach the vegetables in the remaining vinegar for about five minutes.

Pour in the mustard paste, add the sugar, check for seasoning and store in clean, sterilised bottles.

Makes about 1 kilogram pickle

32 How Do You Think I Found My Tahini?

Kodaikanal is my pick for a fabulous getaway. Even with the hillsides being ravaged by construction and the droves of tourists in `season', it keeps its tranquillity and charm in certain hidden nooks. And when I can tear myself away from the wooded trails and the hidden waterfalls, I find myself enjoying the unexpectedness of Kodaikanal's quaint little shops.

There is a lovely bakery, serving fresh cakes and wonderful chicken and mayo sandwiches. And Eco Nut, a shop selling all manner of organic foods. Imagine my pleasure then, at spotting a line-up of tahini jars here. I mean, the stuff isn't that easy to find even in Bangalore. Perhaps it has to do with the international community that has made Kodaikanal home.

Anyway, I picked up more than a few jars to make hummus, a dip I just love. Having told you about that chance discovery, I'm aware tahini isn't always available, so you can do away with it when making hummus. It will miss that sesame nuttiness, but you will still have a dip you will enjoy.

Hummus

1 cup white chickpeas, soaked for 10 hours	1 tsp tahini (if you can find it)
2 garlic cloves	1 tsp lime juice
Salt to taste	2 tbsp olive oil
	Red chilli powder, as required

Pressure-cook the chickpeas till tender. This will take about 20 minutes (five to six whistles) in the pressure cooker.

Drain and reserve the stock for thinning the paste. If you wish to make a super refined hummus you can remove the skins. I always do. But you can leave them on as well.

Allow the chickpeas to cool and process in a blender till smooth, adding the garlic and the salt. If it's too thick, add some of the reserved stock in which the chickpeas was cooked.

Add the tahini and the lemon juice and process again in the blender. Check for seasoning.

Serve in a bowl, drizzled with olive oil and with some chilli powder sprinkled on top. Pita crisps go well with this dip as do vegetable crudités.

Serves 3-4

33 The Best Ribs Ever

When I was just starting off as a food writer in Bombay – and I am eternally grateful to my editors Bachi Karkaria and Malavika Sangghvi who gave me the breaks and encouraged me – every experience was special. I learned about the use of chillies from Chef Ananda Solomon who had just returned after months of research in Mexico. I ate my first softshell crabs, tasted my first Merlot at the Harbour Bar, tucked into pot au feu and sipped on the Beaujolais noveau at a special festival the Oberoi hosted every year.

One dining experience I remember best is at the erstwhile Searock Sheraton. There it was, standing sentinel at the edge of a breakwater. The restaurant I ate at was the revolving one, Palace of the West Empress. Very elegant and sophisticated it was. And the dish I enjoyed the most were these wonderful sweet-salty spare ribs.

I looked up many recipe books, did my own experimenting and here is my recipe for some very tasty ribs. Ideally, they should be grilled. But since the pork we get here isn't always the most tender I braise the ribs first and then finish them in the oven to give them a rich glaze.

Honey and Soy Spare Ribs

10-12 spare ribs
3 tbsp honey
1 tbsp soy sauce
1 tsp minced garlic
Salt to taste
1 tsp Chinese five-spice powder or 1 star anise
1 tsp hoisin sauce (optional)

Ask your butcher to trim and separate the ribs. Clean and pat dry the spare ribs. Mix together all the ingredients for the marinade and marinate the spare ribs for 2-3 hours. Pressure-cook the spare ribs alongwith the marinade for 15 minutes. You will not have to add any water.

Place on a well-greased baking tin and grill at 200°C/400°F/Gas Mark 6 for about 10 minutes. Baste in between with the gravy left in the pressure cooker. The ribs should emerge rich brown and sticky. And delicious.

Serves 2-3

34 A Goan Speciality

In the ten years or so that I spent in Bombay I made some fabulous friends. I've always maintained that Bombay is that kind of place. Perhaps, it's the struggle of life in the city that makes people more empathetic.

On the crowded trains, where even standing space is hard fought for, people form lasting bonds, supporting one another through the arduous journey.

I did not meet Lovina on a train, but she and her husband James were the couple we always went to when our long commute was disrupted in any way – by snapped electric cables, flooded train tracks and other calamities. James is Goan, Lovina East Indian and we quickly became part of their extended families. Every occasion and everyday occurrence called for a big tuck in and soaring spirits, thanks to late-night drinking! At a younger age, when it was possible to crash at 3 am and be at work by 10, these impromptu parties seemed like so much fun.

And what conviviality and camaraderie existed at these gatherings, which often ended with music and dancing, even in the most cramped suburban flat!

Lovina was a tireless hostess and an enthusiastic cook, thinking nothing of making chicken curry or pork sausages for a dozen or more people.

I remember her also for her amazing kindness and caring nature. If we stayed over at her place without preparation she would always hand me a set of unused underwear so I could shower and change for office. But to go back to her cooking, her Mackerel Recheado was the best. Here is how she does it:

Mackerel Recheado

4 medium-sized (approx. 200 gm each) mackerel, cleaned and gutted	6 dried red chillies
	4 garlic cloves
	1 tsp pepper
Juice of half a lime	1 tsp cumin
Salt to taste	½ tsp cloves

½ inch cinnamon	4 tbsp vinegar
A pinch of turmeric powder	Oil for shallow-frying
1 tsp sugar	

Wash the fish well, using a little lime juice and salt, and pat dry. You may choose to keep the heads on if you wish. Make diagonal slits on both sides of the fish.

Grind all the remaining ingredients except oil to a fine paste using the vinegar. Rub the paste into the slits. Allow the fish to marinate for a couple of hours.

Just before serving, heat the oil in a thick-bottomed, shallow pan and place the fish in carefully. Allow to cook on one side. Then turn over carefully. Cook till well browned. Serve as a nibble with beer or alongside rice and curry.

Serves 4

35 The Simplest of Rasams

Though we do make rasam at my place, I got acquainted with the real thing only when I encountered Tam brahm cooking long after I'd left home. My husband's friend Satya, who kept a tiny but impeccably tidy flat in Matunga in Mumbai, was one who'd hold forth on the perfect rasam and what it would take to please the picky Thanjavur Brahmin.

We visited Satya at least once a week, to attend his `sessions' to which all his friends were welcome and they'd be treated to some of his bachelor cooking at the end of the evening. This was in the midst of all the gentle philosophy he'd purvey while KL Saigal played on in the background. And he'd tell Peter Sellers jokes.

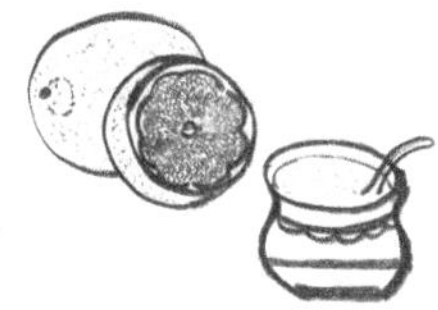

By listening to rasam connoisseurs like that describe the perfect balance that makes this deceptively simple dish, plus my own experimenting, I did manage to come up with a rasam that, to begin with, smelled just right!

I can say with some assurance that I've got very near perfecting the art of making rasam and have quite a repertoire now. If there's going to be no sambar, then I'll make a rasam that's quite thick with dal and tomatoes.

If it's a poor appetite you want to address then, perhaps, a jeera rasam with cumin, tur dal and curry leaves ground together. Sometimes a rasam with lots of garlic does make a great appetiser! But my favourite is the easy-to-make lemon rasam. It's so easy you don't even need rasam powder!

Lemon Rasam

2 tbsp split pigeon peas
1 ripe tomato, peeled and diced
1 tsp ghee
A pinch of mustard seeds
A sprig of curry leaves
1 dried red chilli, broken
A pinch of asafoetida
1 green chilli, finely chopped
½ inch ginger, chopped
Salt to taste
Juice of ½ a lime
A sprig of coriander leaves

Pressure-cook the split pigeon peas with the tomato in a cup of water. Mash the dal to get a soupy consistency.

For seasoning the rasam; heat the ghee in a karhai. Put in the mustard seeds, the curry leaves, the red chilli pieces and the asafoetida. Quickly toss in the green chilli and ginger, and pour into the dal-tomato mixture.

Add another cup of water, salt to taste and bring to a boil. Remove from the heat after two minutes. Pour in the lime juice and sprinkle the coriander leaves.

Eat with soft-cooked rice, adding more ghee if you like, with a nice roasted potato dish, fried papad or vadagam for accompaniment.

Serves 2-3

36 A Very Pondicherry Salad

Pondicherry was an entirely chance discovery for me. A holiday plan had gone awry and I was desperate to get away. So, on a whim, without a plan or any notion of what to expect, I set off for Pondy. I wasn't prepared for the charms of the place.

There it lay, under azure skies and by the turquoise waters, gleaming white – the way one imagines a sunny corner of the Mediterranean to be. The straight grid streets are lined with beautiful homes behind high walls over which the bouganvillea hangs thick and vibrant.

Sometimes an open door will provide you a glimpse of the homes, cool and tree-shaded, built no doubt for the original French inhabitants to be protected from the tropical heat. You wish you could just step in and curl up on a wicker chair with a tall, cool drink.

And the drink flows in Pondicherry. I've spent long afternoons at Seagull, the local tourism department's restaurant which occupies a spectacular spot, the waves just a few feet away from where you sit and knock back the beers or breezers.

It's not particularly well-maintained and the food is all greasy, masala peanuts and stuff like that. But it's simply the most enjoyable way to spend a Pondicherry morning that spills languidly into the afternoon.

But after the drinking we went looking for a place to eat, and ended up at this charming French-style place where you eat at tables covered in red checked table cloths, amid a pretty garden.

They do a pretty nice Coq au Vin and Fish in Lemon Butter – and all the seafood in Pondicherry is fab. But what I had because I wanted to eat light, was this scrumptious salad.

Lettuce, Potato and Bacon Salad

1 bunch lettuce (a combination of romaine, butterhead and iceberg is good)	1 large onion
	1 tbsp olive oil
	2 rashers bacon
	2 tbsp mayonnaise
1 potato	Salt and pepper to taste

Boil the potato till soft. Allow to cool. Cut the potato into thick slices. Set aside. Take the lettuce leaves apart, discarding woody stems and rinse well. Dry well (see below).

Tear into large shreds. Peel the onion. Cut into half and slice into half rings.

Heat the oil in a small pan and sauté the onions lightly. They do not need to cook through, merely lose their raw flavour a little. Lift the onions and set aside.

Cut the bacon into small squares and fry in the same oil till crisp. Lift out and drain on kitchen paper. Just before serving, place the lettuce in a serving bowl, add the onions, bacon and potatoes, put in the mayo and give everything a light toss.

I usually like to thin the mayo with a tablespoon of warm water to make it less rich.

Season with salt and pepper and serve at once as a salad course, or with some crusty bread for a light lunch.

Serves 2

How to Dry Salad Greens

Rinse your greens and shake off excess water. If you have a salad spinner, use it to make the drying of salad greens easy. Otherwise, wrap them loosely in newspaper and place in a bag.

Swing the bag vigorously in circles. Most of the water will be removed and you can proceed to arrange and dress your salad. The swinging bag is unconventional, but works – something about centrifugal forces.

37-38 Mango Chutney, Two Ways

Chatni, they call it in Bengal. And it's the preferred finale to a long lunch of bhaja, bhaat, dal, torkari and maach. How well the Bengalis eat! I came to appreciate the joy of eating like a Bengali during the holidays I spent with my husband in Kolkata in the rambling home of his best friend, Ambar Roy, the cricketer.

Lunch was a celebration that began with instructions from the lady of the house to the trusty old domestic help. He would be ordered to bring two types of fish and the vegetables of the season.

Preparations and the cooking would follow, the vegetables being cut just so, some fried, some combined with the fish and some cooked on their own in the most delicious medleys. And then it would be time to sit down to the repast, to be eaten at a leisurely pace.

First, bhaja or fries with the rice and a little ghee. Then dal and vegetables. The piece de resistance would, of course, be the fish, redolent of mustard oil. I would lick clean the bell metal plates and then have the chutney served on it.

This chutney, usually made from either tomatoes or unripe green mango, is a thick, sweet concoction spiked with Bengali spices. It has the consistency of slightly runny jam and I love to pick up dollops with my fingers and then slurp away. Here is the recipe.

Aamer Chatni from Bengal

2 large unripe green mangoes

1 tbsp mustard oil

1 tsp panch phoron (made by combining equal parts of mustard, cumin, saunf, fenugreek and onion seeds)

1 bay leaf

2 whole red chillies, broken

Salt to taste

1 tbsp sugar

Peel and cut the mango into slivers.

Heat the oil; add the panch phoron, the bay leaf and the chillies. Add the mango; sauté and add enough water to cover and allow the mango to cook till soft.

Stir in the salt and sugar and allow the sugar to melt and form a thick syrup that clings to the mango bits.

Serve at room temperature.

Serves 4-6

Sri Lankan-style Mango Chutney

In Sri Lanka, the mango chutney – hot, sweet and sour – is what they call a rice-puller, something to help you eat more of what's on your plate. The government-run marketing department makes a very good version and bottles of this mango chutney are a great addition to any kitchen. It's great with chapati, puri, even on buttered toast and is fabulous with a Sri Lankan rice and curry meal.

4 large green mangoes
5 dried red chillies
1 tsp mustard seeds
2 garlic cloves
1 inch ginger
1 cup vinegar
1 cup sugar
Salt to taste

Peel and slice the mangoes and dry them for a day in the sun.

Grind together the chillies, mustard seeds, garlic and ginger with half the vinegar.

Dissolve the sugar in the rest of the vinegar. Bring it to a boil; add the ground ingredients and cook to get a syrup consistency.

Add the sliced mangoes and salt and cook for 15 minutes till mango slices are tender.

Allow to cool and store in a sterilised jar.

Serves 4-6

39 A Deceptively Simple Dal

Bread 'n' butter, roti and sabzi, rice and dal – basic and deeply satisfying. Think about it: isn't that what you crave when you want the comfort of familiarity? For me, nothing beats the feel of hot rice and a dal or rasam in my fingers when I'm longing for home food after days of eating adventurously. Rice and dal, it is certainly a pairing ordained by the kitchen gods.

I love all kinds of dal – a simple varan, Maharashtrian-style, the Tam bram paruppu that starts a festive meal, a nice Punjabi dal tadka spiked with garlic. And in Kolkata I came to love mushurir dal which is masur dal cooked in a very simple way. And deliciously satisfying it is, poured over a mound of steaming hot rice.

Mushurir Dal

½ cup split red lentils	2 red chillies, broken
2 tsp mustard oil or ghee	1 small onion, finely chopped
A pinch of onion seeds	½ inch ginger, grated

Wash the lentils. Pressure-cook till soft.

Heat the oil in a thick-bottomed pan and add the onion seeds and the red chillies.

Add the chopped onion and fry till it begins to turn golden. Add the dal and let it simmer briefly. Add the ginger, squeezing the juice into the dal.

Serve hot with rice.

Serves 2

40 Fish That Packs a Punch

It was in Kolkata that I was first introduced to the heavenly pairing between fish and mustard. It was ilish season and there was quite an ado in the Rai-baari about getting a good specimen and cooking it for lunch.

There was *maach bhaja* to begin with, fish oil and then, the piece de resistance, shorshe ilish. There was the sweet, rich fish wrapped in a green-yellow sauce, the richness of the fish cut by the sharpness of the mustard. It was perfect. It's the sort of meal you want to linger over, savouring mouthful after mouthful.

When I get a *shorshe* ilish craving I like to go to one of the Bengali restaurants in Bangalore. The Esplanade in Indiranagar serves up a nice version. I make my version of mustard fish while entertaining at home. It doesn't have to be hilsa. Most fish work well.

Fish in a Mustard Sauce

- 500 gm of fish fillet, seer or pomfrct works well
- 1 tsp salt
- ½ tsp turmeric
- 2 tbsp mustard seeds
- 2 green chillies
- 2 tbsp mustard oil

Clean and wash the fish, rubbing in a little salt and turmeric.

Rinse and pat dry. Arrange in a baking dish. Set aside. Run the mustard seeds through your chutney grinder with the salt. Add the green chillies and a little water and grind to a fine paste.

Strain the mustard paste over the fish. Top with a couple of slit green chillies, drizzle the mustard oil over the fish and cook uncovered in an oven at 180°C/350°F/Gas Mark 4 for about half an hour.

Serve hot with plain rice.

Serves 3-4

41 Winter Oranges

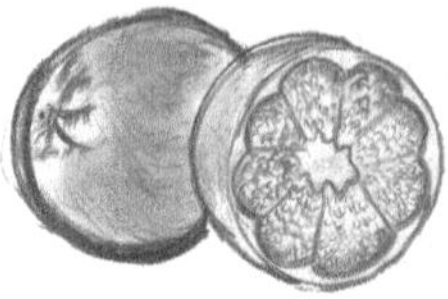

This is a sweet dish I learned to make in Kolkata. It was almost always in the winter that we took our annual breaks in the city. And I think the city, smog-ridden as it used to be, was a culinary delight in the cooler months.

This was also orange season and the Bombay-Kolkata train would pass through Nagpur and it was possible to buy baskets of the fruit at the station.

There is only so much fruit you can eat just like that and so Ambar Roy's lovely wife Tutun (that was her dak naam) who was our hostess would make this wonderful dessert. I had no idea thickened milk and fruit paired so well.

Kheer Kamala

2 litres whole milk

½ cup sugar

Six oranges

Use the best oranges you can find. Pour the milk in a thick-bottomed pan; bring to a boil.

Reduce the heat and allow it to simmer, stirring occasionally. Let the milk reduce to two-third its volume. Add the sugar and allow to cool.

To prepare the oranges, peel and open each segment. Take out the flesh, leaving back the seeds and pith. Do this gently without bruising the fruit too much.

When the milk is completely cool, put in the orange segments. Chill well and serve for dessert after a spicy meal.

Serves 4-6

42 Peas Time

This is another favourite from my wintertime eating in Kolkata. Fresh green peas, sweet and perky are in the market in that season.

And abundance is often turned into a filling for puri. Matarshutir kachori are delicious, calorie-filled breakfast or evening snack. And well worth indulging in when fresh peas are in season.

Matarshutir Kochori

For the Puri/Kochori	For the Filling
2 cups refined flour	2 cups shelled green peas
1 tbsp oil + for deep-frying	1 green chilli
Salt to taste	½ inch ginger
	2 tsp oil
	A pinch of cumin seeds
	A pinch of asafoetida

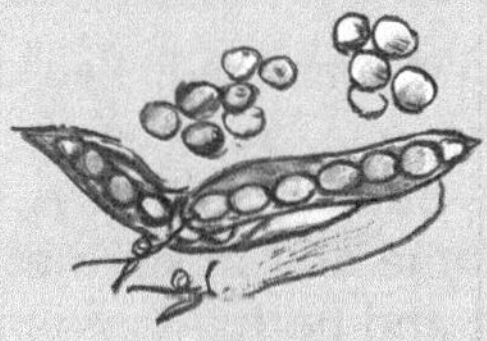

Knead the flour to a soft, pliable dough with about half a cup of water, one tablespoon oil and salt. Set aside.

For the filling, grind the peas with the green chilli and ginger without adding water.

Heat the oil; add the cumin seeds and asafoetida. When the cumin seeds change colour add the ground peas into the pan and sauté till the mixture begins to change colour and becomes crumbly.

To make the kochori, divide the dough into equal portions and roll into lemon-sized balls. Roll each ball into a 4-inch disc.

Place about a tablespoon of the filling, gather the edges together to make a ball; and roll like a puri. Deep-fry in hot oil.

These are usually served with aloo dum, but I like to eat them just like that.

Makes about 10 kachori

43 A Happy Meal-in-One

Whenever I go to Colombo these days, I stay with my cousin who's more like my elder sister. It is to spend time with her that I make these trips. And in her charming flat, made comfortable with all the little touches she puts in – a night person, she's known to rearrange furniture at 1 am or thereabouts – we catch up, talking about our lives, frequently flitting back to the past.

Our reminiscences run along the lines of `Remember those huge bunches of flowers that were sent down from the estates for our birthdays?' and chortle over the various antics of our insane bunch of relatives.

We talk of childhood, growing old, acceptance, sharing our own brand of philosophy. And when we weren't talking I would be cooking. Even before I arrived in Colombo I'd make a mental list of things I'd want to cook for her:

Some old favourites and new dishes I'd mastered. I've always been the more domestic, kitchen-loving one, Saro being `wild' even in her early teens. A real BTDT gal! But now, she says, we've reversed types and it's she who sits home and dusts the plants and rearranges the divan while I go out and party.

Well, that's not always the case. My happiest moments are still bustling about in her nice little kitchen sipping on a beer or glass of wine while I cook. One of the dinners she absolutely loves is the Khau Swey.

I don't even know how authentic it is, never having been to Burma or even eaten it made by a Burmese. Mine is a version inspired by recipe books and my own touches. Still, it's utterly delicious and a great dish for entertaining.

It's simple and still appears very special. The garnishes may seem like a lot of extra work, but do take the trouble. They really add a kick to the final dish!

Khau Swey

For the Garnish

Ingredients	For the Garnish
500 gm boneless chicken, cut into small cubes	One small onion, finely sliced and fried till brown and crisp
1 tbsp oil	One egg, hardboiled and chopped fine
1 large onion, grated	One small bunch coriander leaves, washed and finely chopped
1 inch ginger, grated	1 tbsp red chilli flakes, stirred into 2 tbsp hot oil
6 garlic cloves , crushed	1 lime, cut into wedges
1 tsp cumin-coriander powder	1 tbsp fish sauce with a green chilli sliced into it
½ tsp red chilli powder	A handful of uncooked noodles, deep-fried in oil till golden
2 cups thick coconut milk	
2 tsp fish sauce	
2 packets noodles	

To make the chicken curry, heat the oil in a heavy pan and put in the grated onion, ginger and garlic. Sauté over low heat for 5 minutes or more till the raw flavour disappears. Put in the chicken and stir about.

Add the spice powders and keep frying for about 10 minutes till the meat is coated with the spice mix. Now add 1 cup of coconut milk and one and half cups of water and bring to a boil. Simmer gently for half an hour. Finish with the thick coconut milk and a splash of fish sauce.

Just before serving, reheat the chicken curry over a low heat; cooking the noodles along side. Put the ingredients for garnish in individual small bowls ready for serving.

To serve, dish out the noodles into individual bowls, old-fashioned soup plates are nice – pour the curry over and pass the garnishes around.

Everyone tops their bowls with whatever they like and digs in. This is a great dish to entertain with – not much trouble and very impressive!

Serves 4

44 Pub Grub I Love Best

I was just twenty and it was my first experience of an English summer. The parks were green and the sun shone, well, almost all the time. I went to the National Gallery again and again and filled the gaps in-between, traipsing through Charing Cross.

I went on London Walks, loving the Oscar Wilde one and the London of Dickens and Shakespeare. I was on a very tight budget, so I worked at learning all the `London on the cheap' techniques. I tucked into the big breakfasts at the B&B which fuelled the morning's walking – through Camden Town, Fitzrovia with its homes sporting blue heritage plaques (Virgina Woolf lived here!), and by the Thames. Then scouted around for modest pubs in the late afternoon. I loved pub grub, having to make only simple choices: fried fish, bangers or pork chops. And the girls always asked, `Chips or mash, peas or beans?' It's been made fun of and ridiculed. It's the stuff of jokes. But I loved bangers and mustard mash.

And then I went to Stratford-upon-Avon, on a cloudless, blue-sky day. The willows wept into the still river and the swans preened in the sun. It was also a day when the place teemed with tourists.

The pubs and restaurants were packed. I don't remember the name of the pub, but I know it was crowded, they barely managed to squeeze in a table in a sort of corridor. But who cared, for the shepherd's pie was the best! It's something I like to bake on a cold evening. Put it together in the morning. And after a long day, all you have to do is pop it in the oven and pour yourself a beer while it bakes to a golden-topped treat.

Shepherd's Pie

400 gm lean mince (lamb or beef)
1 tbsp oil
1 large onion, finely chopped
2-3 garlic cloves, chopped
200 gm tomato, peeled and chopped
A pinch of mixed herbs
Salt and pepper to taste
A dash of Worcestershire sauce
400 gm potato
200 ml warm milk
50 gm butter

To make the meat filling, heat the oil in a thick-bottomed pan; add the onion and garlic, and sauté gently till the onion is translucent; add the mince and sauté till it loses its redness.

Add the tomato, the herbs, salt and pepper to taste and sauté for a few minutes.

Cover and let the meat cook till tender. It should all be wrapped in a rich, thick gravy. Add the Worcestershire sauce.

To make the topping, peel and cut the potatoes into large chunks and cook in salted water till tender. Drain.

Mash the cooked potatoes and add the warm milk and the butter. Mix well. Season with the salt and pepper.

To assemble the pie, place the meat in an oven-proof dish that's about 4-inch deep, spread the mashed potato on top, giving it a rough surface and bake at 200°C/400°F/Gas Mark 6 till the top is golden.

Serve with a salad or some green veggies such as steamed beans.

Serves 2-3

45 Biryani for a Crowd

My brother, like most Indian boys, didn't enter the kitchen as a child or teenager, leave alone make coffee or boil an egg. But having lived away from home for many years, and thanks to his abiding love of good food, he's turned out to be that one thing that makes a man extra attractive: a superlative cook. This, I discovered, the first night of my first visit to him in Oslo, where he now lives with my sister-in-law and three kids. Jet-lagged, I rested while he got busy in the kitchen. I woke up to the heavenly aroma of roasting lamb. It tasted better than it smelled and with a red wine sauce and roast potatoes it made for a meal I shall never forget. Now, it's a sort of a tradition.

Every time I visit my brother, on the evening of my arrival and just before I leave, he makes his roast lamb, studded with garlic, rubbing the seasoning and olive oil into the meat and leaving it to marinate for 12 hours or so. Then he roasts it in his cavernous oven for several hours and whips up a brilliant sauce or two – either the wine sauce I spoke of before or a fabulous blue cheese one. And he calls all his friends over for a real big feast.

My brother and sister-in-law keep open house in Oslo. I guess it is their way of ensuring warmth and a sense of home in faraway Scandinavia. So, as it happens, there are always friends walking in expecting a satisfying meal. Weekends see the crowds swell and if my sis-in-law is making dosa or idiappam then the phone calls go out well in advance and everyone arrives ready for a big tuck-in. Special occasions see a table laden with Norwegian specialities and Indian food. One Christmas, for instance, we dined on the Norwegian yuletide fare of ribbe or stack of pork ribs with crackling on one side and biryani on the other. It's a challenge to cook for a crowd but my sister-in-law is something of an expert. And this biryani, which she makes in two parts and then assembles, is a little unconventional but very, very good.

Mutton Biryani

1 kg good quality mutton
500 ml yogurt
3 tbsp ginger-garlic paste
1 tbsp red chilli powder
2 tbsp coriander powder
2 tbsp cumin powder

1 kg Basmati rice	1 tbsp whole cardamom
100 ml ghee	1 tbsp black cardamom
5 onions, finely sliced	1 tbsp cloves
400 gm ripe tomatoes, chopped	4 one-inch cinnamon sticks
	1 cup chopped coriander leaves
Salt to taste	½ cup chopped mint leaves

Marinate the mutton in the mixture of yogurt, the ginger-garlic paste and the dry spices. (Instead of the spice powders, you could use a good biryani masala as well.) Marinate for 3 hours.

Wash the rice well and soak for an hour or so.

Heat half the ghee in a thick-bottomed pan; add half the onions and deep-fry till golden brown.

Add the tomatoes, sauté till pulpy. Add the mutton with the marinade, stir well, add salt to taste and cover and cook for about an hour till mutton is tender. Alternatively, pressure-cook for three whistles to speed up the process.

To make the rice, heat the remaining ghee, put in the whole spices and the remaining onions. Sauté on low heat till the onions begin to change colour.

Add the rice and the coriander leaves and mint leaves. Sauté till the rice is well-coated with the ghee. Pour in enough hot water to come up to two inches above the rice. Add salt to taste. Cover and cook till quite tender. Do not overcook the rice.

When the meat and the rice are both done, add the rice to the meat and stir gently. The biryani is now ready to serve.

It is an especially good method when you have to cook for a big group and don't have large enough vessels to make it all at one go. Double the quantity of rice and meat for a big group.

If you are serving fewer people, then spread the rice on top of the cooked mutton, cover and leave on a low heat for about 10 minutes.

Serves 6-8

46 Clever Use of Leftovers

My teenager nephew in Oslo is a very keen cook. He's had cooking lessons in school and loves to test his skills in the kitchen. Mahish is also quite an expert on Norwegian dishes and ingredients.

He's a young gourmet with quite adventurous taste buds – willing to try sashimi, Argentinian beef, strong cheeses. He's not an easy young man to impress. But on a cold Oslo morning I made him breakfast from leftovers and he was.

A pasta omelette or frittata is really an excellent way to use leftover pasta – whether a carbonara or spaghetti bolognaise. If it's already packed with meats, cheese and veggies, you don't need to add much more.

Just the eggs and you have a substantial omelette. For young Mahish I used leftovers from the dinner of pasta with cheese and veggies. We were just back from our trip to Florence and had brought back a hunk of mortadella, some of which I added to the spaghetti omelette. It was, as Mahish will vouch, a super brunch dish.

Pasta Omelette

2 tbsp butter	4 eggs
A soup bowl full of leftover pasta	Salt and pepper to taste
	1 tbsp fresh herbs, chopped

Melt the butter in an omelette pan. Put in the pasta and spread out. Beat the eggs with the salt and pepper. Pour over the pasta and cook over medium heat till the top is fairly set. Turn over carefully and let the other side cook.

Serve hot with buttered toast.

If your pasta is quite plain to begin with, you can sauté some chopped onion in the butter, add cold meat such as ham, the herbs and then put in the pasta and pour the egg over. Grate on more cheese if you like as well.

Serves 2

47 Memories of Oslo in Summer

Ah Oslo! How I love the city I've grown quite accustomed to, thanks to the yearly visits to my brother. Snow-bound for most part of the year, it has its wintry charms. But there's no doubt that this sparkling city shows off its best side in the brief summer.

That is when Akerbrygge the fjordside development and one of the city's favourite public spaces, reverberates with all the brightness and colour of the season.

In a remarkable example of combining a city's heritage with utility, a string of old warehouses along the waterfront has been converted into a space housing options for shopping, recreation, eating and drinking.

Akerbrygge is a must-do in Oslo for shopping, savouring a bowl of moules meuniere or stopping by for a beer or simply strolling. An old ship anchored at Akerbrygge is now a chic bar and restaurant, a great place for hanging by the rails sipping bellinis and looking across the water at the imposing Akershus castle.

One summer, there was a promo for Norwegian seafood here. A band played and crowds gathered under the white tents to savour mussels, shrimp and the very best salmon, cooked while they watched. Norwegian salmon, of course, needs no introduction.

Right off the waters, it's the most beautiful pink, rich and moist when cooked right. Norwegians either poach the fish or grill it simply with lemon and a scattering of dill. And I cannot think of a better way to cook this delightful fish.

If you feel like splurging, do use salmon which is sometimes available in gourmet stores and hypermarkets here. Else, Indian salmon or rawas works fine.

Fish with Lemon Butter

4 fillets or slices salmon or rawas

Salt and freshly ground pepper to taste

Juice of 2 lemons

A few sprigs of dill

4 tbsp butter

A few steamed baby potatoes

Toss the fish with half the lemon juice, salt and pepper to taste.

Place each slice on a square foil, top with a few fronds of the dill, fold the foil to form a parcel and grill at 200°C/400°F/Gas Mark 6 for about 12 minutes. The fish should be cooked through, but not overdone.

For the lemon-butter, melt the butter in a pan, and add the remaining lemon juice. Serve the fish with the lemon-butter poured over and some boiled or steamed baby potatoes on the side.

Serves 2

48 Fried Rice without Rules

I do love fried rice. I can eat any sort and, preferably, without accompaniments. I remember my first taste of fried rice; it was what my dad would sometimes bring us after work as a late night treat. It was wrapped in greaseproof paper and had little shrimps in it. And it smelled wonderful. Then, there's the Sri Lankan version, with all the veggies fried in butter and the rice tossed in. Nothing like the Chinese dish, but delightful nevertheless. It was a frequent packed lunch for school.

But then I ate in authentic Chinese restaurants and came to know real good fried rice. From Kylie Kwong's show I've learned a good fried rice must have only scrambled eggs and shallots. No baby corn and other crunchy bits. But to my mind a good fried rice is whatever you want it to be, with lots of flavourful ingredients in it. Thailand has some fabulous fried rice dishes and I remember a seafood one eaten in a riverside restaurant by the Kwai which will always count among the best I've tasted. I suspect it had MSG in it, as do many dishes in Thai eateries, but what the heck. With those chunks of seafood, all fragrant and hot, with a scattering of chillies it was wonderful.

My fried rice recipe is very variable, depending on my mood and the ingredients at hand. This one has many bits and pieces in it and is nice and spicy, too.

Spicy Fried Rice

2 cups rice, cooked and cooled
½ cup pork or chicken, cut into small dices
1 cup peeled shrimps
3-4 garlic cloves
½ inch, fresh ginger, peeled
1 tsp chilli flakes
2 tbsp oil
2 eggs, lightly beaten with a pinch of salt
½ cup French beans, sliced
1 small bunch spring onions, cleaned and finely sliced
1 tbsp fish sauce
A handful of fresh basil leaves

It is essential that the rice is cooked tender, not mushy, and then thoroughly cooled. Then get the other ingredients together.

Marinate the pork and shrimp separately, with salt, pepper and a dash of fish sauce.

Process the garlic, ginger and chilli flakes with a little water to make a coarse paste in a blender. The other crucial element to good fried rice is a thick-bottomed pan that is really hot and a high heat to keep it so.

Pour a tablespoon of oil into the pan, pour in the eggs and scramble. Transfer and place on the rice. Heat the remaining oil, add the spice paste and sauté for a minute or so. Add the pork or chicken, then the shrimps and stir on high heat till done.

Add the French beans and when they are done, add the spring onions. You should work fast or you will have a soggy mess.

Now put in the rice and the eggs, stir everything together, adding the fish sauce and, at last, the basil leaves. Eat hot. You won't need any accompaniments for this hearty dish.

Serves 2-3

49 Tea, Anyone?

Singapore isn't my favourite place on earth. The disciplined traffic and all the manicured greenery are not agreeable to my chaos-loving spirit. They say the shopping's great, but every time I've browsed or touched something in a display there's been an annoying salesperson in an Esprit T-shirt saying `200 sing dolah' and I've simply fled the place. The tourist attractions like the `world's tallest man-made waterfall' (c'mon I've seen better) leave me cold. But the food, now that's a different matter. For Singapore is truly a melting pot of cuisines. To eat out here is to be dazzled by the sheer variety.

At the high end of the scale there are brilliant chefs from across the world who come here to showcase their flair. I have tasted the creations of Chef Susur Lee from Canada at the Club Chinois and the classic fare at the Goodwood hotel where you eat with chopstick pairs joined with gold-plated chains. Every expensive taste is catered to in this gourmet heaven, every whim and culinary fancy satisfied.

It doesn't always have to be upscale and pricey. At the other end there are the hawker markets now completely sanitised and still offering a mind-boggling range of local delicacies, from congee to Hainanese chicken and ice kachang. In-between there are row upon row of restaurants serving Singapore's special delights. The ethnic quarters, despite being much-hyped tourist destinations, are places where you can chance upon some superlative food.

The Indian, rather Tamil, quarter is showcased as one of the colourful aspects of Singapore life; there are garland stalls, 'fancy' stores selling trinkets from India and DVD shops stocking all the latest Tamil blockbusters. Then there's the famous Komala Vilas and a whole host of shops selling idli, vadai and dosai. These I did not venture into for obvious reasons. What I did discover was the charms of the tea-house in Singapore's China Town. Here, I learned the ancient art of drinking tea, ceremoniously, in delicate porcelain cups and sampled a range of fine teas. There was a small food menu, too, and it offered up a dish, the taste of which I have never forgotten. It was a whole chicken, which appeared at the table, most unpretentiously, wrapped in foil. The foil was pulled open and there it was, a most attractive shade of rich brown, acquired from the tea leaves that had been rubbed all over it. Other Chinese herbs and roots, including ginseng, form the flavouring for this remarkable dish. Apparently, it is rubbed over with the tea and other condiments, salted and then wrapped in foil and steamed gently. The result is tender meat with a most intriguing flavour and remarkable aroma. The meat is succulent and wonderful and what's more it releases a flavourful, golden broth.

A small bowl of steamed rice and quick fried bok choy is all you need to complement this Chinese classic. Of course, I do not have access to all the splendid Chinese ingredients, but I came up with a practical version of this dish and you will love it, too.

Tea-steamed Chicken

1 whole (approx. 1.5 kg) chicken	2 inches ginger, sliced
Salt to taste	5 whole dried red chillies
2 tbsp premium tea, such as Darjeeling	3-4 star anise
	A few drops of soy sauce

The chicken should be skinless and giblets removed. Wash and pat dry inside and out. Rub with salt all over.

Take a piece of heavy-duty kitchen foil, large enough to hold the chicken in the centre. Place the bird in the middle, scatter over the tea leaves, the ginger, the chillies, star anise and drizzle the soy sauce on top.

Wrap the chicken in the foil to make a well-sealed parcel. Steam gently for 45 minutes. If you have a proper steamer, that would be perfect. I sometimes placed the chicken in foil in a deep heat-proof bowl and place that in a larger vessel with water in it. Then cover the whole and place it on the heat. At the end of the cooking time, lift out the parcel and serve directly, with no more than some steamed rice and stir-fried Chinese greens.

You carve the chicken at the table and also scoop up some of the broth which has formed around it. This is how it's usually done, for this is a no-fuss dish. Still, if you want to do it differently, you could carve the chicken, place it on a serving plate and strain the broth over it.

Serves 4

50 A River-side Delicacy

I have confessed that most of Singapore's hard-sold attractions leave me cold, but it's true too that I have had an awfully good time in the place. It is in Singapore that I appreciated the pleasure of going anywhere with the perfect travel companion.

On this particular trip I was invited to view the launch of a sound and light extravaganza on Sentosa island. After that, my friend and I were free to take in all the fun that this fantasy island offered. We hung out at Vivo City mall, ate in all manner of restaurants there – from sushi places to an excellent Argentinian grill.

We rode the cable car and did other fun things. Then we explored the malls, but of course, and little out-of-the-way shops as well. Our big splurge was a quiet, candle-lit evening at Chijmes, a cloister converted into a bouquet of food and wine options. And which traveller can resist the lure of Clarke Quay.

Here, we spent a long and wonderful evening pub-hopping and eventually wound up on a boat restaurant for dinner. I ate a superlative oyster omelette and then, for main course, a tilapia fished out of the tank, quickly dipped in flour and deep-fried. It put the highlight on a perfect evening, the sort that is not easily conjured up.

My friend and travel companion of the time and I have drifted apart since. But whenever I think of fun times in Singapore, I remember that very special person. But enough of nostalgia.

Here is the recipe for the whole fried fish, Oriental-style.

Whole Fried Fish

- 1 whole snapper or pomfret
- ½ cup flour
- Salt to taste
- Oil for deep-frying
- 2 tsp soy sauce
- 2 tsp sesame oil
- Whole sprigs of green coriander

Gut and clean the fish, keeping the head and tail intact. Wash and pat dry.

Season the flour with the salt and then toss the fish in the flour till it is coated. Heat the oil in a frying pan large enough to hold the whole fish.

Lower the fish carefully into the oil, let it cook on one side for about five minutes, then turn over gently and let both sides turn a nice crispy brown.

Remove from the pan; drain on kitchen paper and place on a serving plate. Drizzle the soy sauce and sesame oil over, scatter the coriander sprigs over the fish and serve hot.

Serves 1 as a main course

51 A Pick-me-Up Bowl

For some people Bangkok is the shopping, for others the massages. For me, it's simply the food. Not in the fancy places or skyscraper restaurants – but on the streets and in the food courts.

The food courts are a far cry from those in our malls. They offer a mind-boggling array of food – from braised pork knuckle to roast duck, seafood fried rice, pad thai and a wonderful line-up of soups – all at very affordable prices.

It's my friend Pat who took me on my first round of a food court in Bangkok, and what a trip that was! We ate salads, stir-fried squid, roast duck, morning glory with fish sauce and several bowls of soup.

Every counter stocked vast bunches of fresh coriander and basil, chilli powder, salt and sugar and you could perk up your soup any way you liked. I love a spicy Thai-style soup with noodles and lots of aromatics in it.

Here is the one I make at home when I'm sorely in need of a pick-me-up. At the heart of it is a good stock:

Chicken Noodle Soup

For the Chicken Stock

- 500 gm chicken bones
- 2 celery stalks
- 1 inch ginger or galangal
- 1 tsp dried kafir lime leaves
- 2 inches lemon grass

Put the bones and the other ingredients into 2 litres of water, bring to a boil.

Reduce heat and allow to simmer for about 3 hours.

The idea is to get a stock that has extracted all the flavour from the bones and the aromatics. Skim away any scum that rises to the surface.

Strain and use for soup.

For the Soup

- 4 cups chicken stock
- 1 cup noodles, cooked
- 200 gm cooked chicken, shredded
- A dash of fish sauce
- 2 tsp lime juice
- 1 green chilli, finely chopped
- Salt to taste
- Black pepper powder to taste
- A handful of bean sprouts
- 1 sprig of basil leaves

Bring the stock to a boil; add the noodles, chicken, fish sauce, lime juice and the chilli. Adjust the salt and pepper.

Pour into soup bowls and serve topped with bean sprouts and basil leaves in individual bowls.

Serves 2-3

52 From the Italian Riviera

I went to Florence a couple of years ago and fell under its spell. Who can fail to be moved by the sights of this city, the birthplace of the Renaissance. There is the cathedral and its much-photographed dome, the Uffizi gallery, the Pitti palace, the sculptures of Michelangelo and the graceful architecture at every turn.

Then there are the lesser known squares and piazzas and the splendid bistros and restaurants. For breakfast I ate superb prosciutto on beautiful rolls and drank freshly squeezed orange juice. The lamb and beef were excellent everywhere and I drank copious quantities of Chianti from the Tuscan Hills around.

It was nearly the end of summer and the slopes were turning colour. The views across the river Arno and its many bridges, particularly the Ponte Vecchio, are not easily matched. And then, my brother, adventurous traveller that he is, suggested we hop on a train and explore the region surrounding this magnificent city.

We bought train tickets to La Spezia and, once there, on a whim, took a bus to the coast. It drove up winding cliffs through olive groves – this is on the Ligurian coast and producer of some of the world's best olive oil. And then plunged down to the coast. Porto Venere took my breath away, the wild sea pounding against magnificent, jagged rock formations and mysterious grottos.

It was off-season, so the little town with its high-fronted pastel coloured houses, which make you think of the squares in a paint box, was quite quiet. By the sea were a string of tavernas and restaurants serving simple Italian fare, their speciality being seafood. We ate in one of these overlooking the marina with its bobbing yachts. We tucked into fresh sardines, squid and then a fabulous seafood pasta – rich and creamy, and packed with sweet crabmeat. Later we strolled about in and out of souvenir shops.

At one, I bought some of the local, handpainted pottery and the woman gave me a freebie. It was a little pottery slab, the shape of a small bat. It has three round holes of different sizes in it. For measuring spaghetti, she told me, `per une persona, per due persone et per tre'. Here goes my version of seafood pasta:

Tagliatelle with Seafood

500 gm tagliatelle

500 gm seafood (use a mix of prawns, cubes of boneless fish, squid rings and small shrimp)

6 garlic cloves

4 tbsp olive oil

500 gm tomatoes, peeled and chopped

½ glass white wine

Salt to taste

½ tsp chilli flakes

½ cup parsley, chopped

Clean and prepare the fish and shellfish. Peel and chop the garlic fine. Heat the olive oil in a thick-bottomed pan, and add the garlic, stir for a few seconds and add the tomatoes. Sauté for a few minutes and add the wine. Allow most of it to evaporate and add the seafood and fish.

Add salt to taste and the chilli flakes. Let the sauce simmer away until the seafood is all cooked through.

While the sauce is simmering cook the pasta in a large pot of salted water. Finish the sauce with chopped parsley. Strain the pasta, toss with the sauce and serve hot.

Serves 4

Variation

Alternatively, you can leave out the tomatoes, sauté the seafood, add a little fish stock and white wine, finish with a dash of cream and a sprinkling of saffron.

53 A Chic French Appetiser

My trip to the Champagne region, thanks to a media outing arranged by champagne ambassador Rajiv Singhal who now also publishes a fine magazine on wines, was one of the most rewarding for me as a food and wine writer.

We were in Rheims right in the middle of the harvest and received first-hand experience picking pinot noir in a small vineyard. We visited several champagne houses – small and big -- with a tour of the famous Veuve Cliquot cellars.

I loved most the trips to the small houses such as Cattier. And I distinctly remember Vollereux which is where I first met Catherine Carey Remonnay who is now one of my best friends.

In Champagne we were invited to chateaux and ate in fine restaurants where I also tasted my first escargot. The flamboyant Bruno Paillard, after showing us around his hi-tech champagne making facility, invited us to his warm and charming home.

We drank the Paillard rosé and then it was a simple, elegant dinner – a starter, fish with wild mushrooms and cheeses and fruit. The first course with the Cherry Tomato Tart left me most impressed.

I asked Mme Paillard how it was made and have since then made my own version.

Cherry Tomato Tart

For the Pastry

150 gm flour

Salt to taste

75 gm butter

For the Topping

2 tbsp tapenade

200 gm cherry tomatoes, halved

To make the pastry, sift the flour with the salt. Rub the butter into the flour till the mixture resembles breadcrumbs.

Pour in 3 to 4 tablespoon iced water gradually and knead lightly. Wrap in cling film and chill for about an hour in the refrigerator.

Just before baking, take the pastry out of the refrigerator and roll out into an 8-inch disc and about ¼-inch thick.

Spread with tapenade. If you cannot find readymade tapenade, use pesto. Or, at a pinch, purée half a cup of green and black olives in the blender and mix into a smooth paste with 2 tbsp of olive oil.

Arrange the cherry tomatoes neatly on the disc, cut side down, and bake at 180°C/350°F/Gas Mark 4 till the pastry is crisp and golden. Cut into wedges and serve.

Serves 2-3

54 With Your Champagne

I think it's a small miracle how we chance upon people in the most unexpected places and then let our lives intertwine. It's what happened to me in Rheims on the tour of the champagne region I told you about.

One particular day, we had visited several champagne houses and gone through even more tastings. At the end of it, even someone who absolutely loves champagne like me could not face another glass.

But the way media tours go, we had one more place to visit before we wound up for the day. The tour group moaned at the prospect, as we arrived at Vollereux one of the region's small but hugely respected champagne makers.

I took a look at the blonde, blue-eyed woman who was promoting their wines and interacting with us and her enthusiasm was infectious. Never mind, if we'd already tasted way too much champagne, I dived right into Cathy's tasting.

The rest of the group begged off after a few sips. But in that ancient winery, on a mellow evening Cathy and I sat and finished the better part of a bottle of Vollereux rose, which is a beautiful champagne, by the way.

I don't know if it was the effect of talking over champagne or Cathy's love of India and her open manner, but we bonded instantly. And we have remained friends since. Usual visits of this nature end with promises to keep in touch and meet, never to be kept, but Cathy and I have remained close despite the distance.

Whenever she visits Bangalore – she has been working on a business to bring quality French wines to India – we spend as much time as possible together. We go bar-hopping, shopping in Com Street, discuss men and have a fun girls' time out.

One day, we decided on a champagne morning with a light repast at Cathy's serviced apartment here. She had put together, simply but elegantly, slices of smoked salmon on buttered brown bread and strawberries sprinkled with soft sugar.

My contribution was poached prawns with a homemade mayonnaise. It's inspired from one by Mireille Guiliano who became famous with her book, *French Women Don't Get Fat*. My French friend approved; here is the recipe:

Homemade Mayo

1 egg yolk	⅔ cup sunflower oil
1 tsp Dijon mustard	Salt to taste
2 tsp white wine vinegar	Freshly ground pepper to taste

Rinse a bowl with hot water. Dry the bowl and place in it the egg yolk, mustard and vinegar. Whisk till combined. Now add the oil a drop at a time, whisking after each addition.

When you've added half the oil, the mixture should be thick and creamy. Add the rest of the oil in a steady stream, whisking constantly.

Add salt and pepper to taste. Store in a glass container. This will keep for 3-4 days in the refrigerator.

Serve with prawns poached gently in stock, or even water. A dash of white wine enhances the flavour considerably.

The mayo is also lovely over steamed asparagus.

Makes about ½ a cup

55 A Parisian Snack

My first view of Paris was on a grey, drizzly day. The metros were crowded, it was freezing and windy and I was hungry. Still, there was the Eiffel Tower to see and off we went.

Later, we dined in a bistro, avoiding the touristy spots and looking for a place where the locals were eating their lunch. I had escargot – in its parsley-flecked garlic butter and a terrine of duck, followed by the perfect crème brûlée. And then, playing the good tourist, it was off to the Louvre and the Notre Dame cathedral.

The Seine, the graceful bridges and the pontoons on the water sure make for a lovely sight. And after all that pounding through the Louvre, it was time for another small meal. What else, but café and crêpes.

We ate ours at a small café in the shadow of the cathedral and I marvelled at the dexterity with which the girl made them wafer thin and lovely.

Mine was citron aux sucre. Through some trial and error my crêpes turn out quite nice, too. Top it with Nutella if you are a chocoholic.

Crêpes

1 cup refined flour
2 cups milk
1 egg, beaten
1 tbsp sugar
3 tbsp melted butter

Put all the ingredients into a large bowl and beat with a hand whisk till you have a thin, lump-free batter.

Set aside for half an hour. When ready to serve the pancakes, heat a heavy griddle or tawa. Pour in a ladleful of batter and spread the batter thin.

Once the surface is cooked, remove carefully, sprinkle with lime and sugar, jam or chocolate spread, fold and serve right away.

Makes about 8 crêpes

56 Tapas Bar Special

Barcelona gets effortlessly on to my list of best cities. What more could you ask for than to while the hours away on La Ramblas. Tourist-infested it may be, but how enjoyable it is to people-watch from a tapas bar, sipping on the clearest sangria, or wander amid the showmen, the jugglers and the musicians.

There are the museums, the beautiful marina, the bonbon stores and, of course, the Gaudi architecture at every turn. While everyone flocks to the Sagra Familia, I was smitten by the grace and beauty of the Santa Maria del Mer. It was in the shadow of this ancient church that we ate some of the best food I had in Barcelona. In one of the alleys was tucked a place where the locals ate. The tapas were fab and I will always remember the baby squid braised simply in a tomato sauce, the razor clams and the pile of julienned vegetables fried crisp in olive oil.

We followed that up with a superlative paella. The recipe that follows is my celebration of the Spanish tapas experience. Made with some real fresh prawns, it's wonderful. It's a fab thing to serve with drinks or as a light meal with, perhaps, a green salad on the side.

Gambas al Ajillo

500 gm super-fresh prawns
50 ml olive oil
50 gm garlic, finely chopped
1 tsp chilli flakes
1 tbsp cognac (optional)
Coarse salt to taste
2 tbsp parsley, chopped

Clean and devein the prawns. Keep the tails on. Heat the oil in a pan, throw in the garlic, do not let it burn. Quickly put in the chilli flakes and add the prawns.

Sauté till the prawns change colour. Add the cognac if using and let it reduce. Put in the salt. Turn off the heat and sprinkle the parsley over.

Serve with plenty of crusty bread to mop up the delicious juices.

Serves 2-3

57 From My Favourite Market

I'm a market junkie. When I go to Colombo I love poking about the fish stalls and the ones selling all manner of lovely greens like cancun and gotukola – a sort of bitter watercress.

On my trips to Madurai I always try to fit in an early morning at the uzhavar sandhai or farmers market to buy small brinjals, wedges of freshly cut pumpkin and banana flowers.

When I used to go to Kolkata regularly, a morning at the markets with the koi leaping about and fresh prawns wriggling in buckets of water was something I would never miss.

In Singapore, as part of a media tour, I was booked into a swish hotel, but once the organised tours and programmes were over, off I went to explore the backlanes and found a market selling a mind-boggling array of dried mushrooms, herbs and roots, besides tea eggs and noodles.

In Phuket my brother and I spent hours in a market, looking at the blinking frogs and the writhing snakes in their cages with some misgiving. But there were beautiful things, too – mountains of tropical fruits and vegetables and vats of spice pastes for Thai curry.

The markets in the souks of Marrakesh and Essaouira are a delight, too – with their pyramids of spice powders and Mediterranean produce. But of all the markets I've been to, the one I most long to return to is the Mercat de Sant Josep de la Boqueria or simply La Boqueria.

Situated just off the tourist hotspot of La Ramblas, La Boqueria is a wonderland of a market with a world-class array of fresh produce, seafood, poultry and meats. Ferran Adria shops here, if you must know.

The mountains of glistening fruit and vegetable in the stall near the entrance alone are enough to leave you bedazzled, until a fearsome shopkeeper tells you not to touch the white truffles.

The meat and poultry stalls are riveting and I was so excited to see a chicken cut open with its string of golden eggs inside. When is the last time we saw that, subjected to eating broilers as we are?

Then there were the stalls stocked with whole Iberian hams, pork cheeks and cured sausages. The egg shops stocking everything from quail eggs to emu eggs, the olives, the olive oils, the spice stalls – oh it was such a feast for the senses, it left you gasping for breath.

And after we did the rounds of the stalls, bought some olive oil and paella spices, we chanced upon a crowded quarter. This was a seafood stall and tapas bar. You could pick your baby squid, shrimp or fish and have it fried, braised or grilled.

Copious quantities of alcohol were being consumed and everyone was having such a good time, we simply had to join the crowd.

The recipe that follows is inspired by the seafood stall in La Boqueria.

Flash-fried Squid

1 kg small squid
Plain flour to dredge
Salt and pepper to taste
Oil for deep-frying

Have your fish-monger clean and gut the squid. If the grey skin is not removed, you will have to pull that off.

Wash well inside and out and pat dry. Cut into fairly thin rings. Put the flour on a sheet of paper, season with the salt and pepper and toss the squid rings in this.

Pick up handfuls and deep-fry in hot oil. They don't take more than 4-5 minutes to cook.

Drain and serve hot with an aioli.

Serves 3-4

58 Cooking Lessons in Marrakesh

After watching all the travel and food shows on Marrakesh's Djemaa El Fnaa, there I was, standing in the famous square, all agog at the sights, the sounds, not to mention the smells of the night market.

The whole place comes to life with fortune tellers and henna artists, raconteurs and acrobats holding the milling crowds in thrall. Then there are the famous food stalls – dozens upon dozens of them – at which I ventured to try snail soup, brochettes of seafood, grilled meats and offal, breads and freshly squeezed orange juice. It's cheap, it's cheerful and it's a true taste of Marrakesh. But beyond this no-frills eating, there are options to explore the more elegant aspects of Moroccan cooking. It is a rich cuisine reflecting the many influences this North African county has imbibed – from Arabic, to Berber and Spanish.

It relies on an abundance of fresh produce from the region – olives and olive oil, superb citrus fruits, aubergines, artichokes and very good meat and seafood. The breads are in a class of their own and then there are the pastilles, the flaky pies with pigeon or game filling, the fragrant stews, the Tangiers of beef and the textured soups. The tagine is, of course, the best known and possibly the easiest to put together for someone just approaching Moroccan food.

I took my first steps by signing up for a cooking class at a riad. The riads are an intrinsic part of the Moroccan life. These wondrous homes lie in the narrow alleys of the old cities, behind heavy doors. Open and you enter a place of untrammelled quiet and serenity. The living quarters are arranged around a courtyard, often paved with marble, with fountains and orange and pomegranate trees. Many of these have now been turned into small luxury hotels and a stay in one is a must-do Morocco experience.

At the beautifully appointed Riad el Zohar with views of the Atlas mountains from its terrace, I learned the basics of Moroccan cuisine from Saida. She spoke no English, so we got by with my faltering French. There was a trip to the poultry market and then the vegetable market at the beginning of the day. Then she taught me how to make two Moroccan salads – one with aubergines and the other with long, green peppers. The main course was chicken with preserved lemons and olives and couscous made from scratch.

Saida steamed it thrice, aerating after each steaming by running the delicate grains through her fingers. Later we dined in the courtyard of the Riad el Zohar on what we had cooked and it's one of the best meals I've ever had.

After that, it was off to Essaouira to discover the charms and the food of this coastal city. En route I stopped in Safi, famed for its glazed pottery, to buy myself a tagine.

It travelled back well and I can now make tagines and couscous for friends. But you can make this dish of chicken and olives in any thick-bottomed pan. And I recommend instant couscous which makes life pretty simple. So do have a Moroccan meal sometime.

Moroccan-style Chicken

- 1 whole (approx. 1.5 kg) chicken, cut into 6 serving pieces
- 2 large onions, grated
- 4 garlic cloves, minced
- 1 inch ginger, grated
- A pinch of turmeric powder
- 4 tbsp olive oil
- 1 tbsp cumin powder
- 1 tbsp coriander powder
- ½ tsp cinnamon powder
- Freshly ground peppercorns to taste
- Salt to taste
- ½ cup stoned olives
- 1 preserved lemon or lemon pickle in brine

Wash and pat dry the chicken.

Put the chicken and all the ingredients except the olives and preserved lemon into a large pan. Bring to a boil; reduce the heat and allow to simmer for an hour or so. The chicken should be cooked through with a fragrant thick sauce around it.

Wash and dry the olives and the preserved lemon or the lemon pickle to remove excess saltiness. Chop olives and lemon into small pieces.

Add the olives and lemon to the chicken, simmer for five minutes and serve with couscous or with baguette to mop up the sauces.

This chicken is even better if made ahead and reheated. Serve in a wide decorative platter for a true Moroccan touch.

Serves 4

59 For a Special Dinner

This little anecdote turned out, unwittingly, like the crux of a novel (or perhaps it was only a novella) I once dreamed of writing. It was, in my foolish enthusiasm and limited literary capacity, to be a Mills & Boon meets Laura Esquivel-like effort.

The heroine would be a passionate cook who would lose her love of her craft because of a personal tragedy, I hadn't gotten down to figuring out quite what.

Enter Mr Perfect and, voila! our heroine would become Julia Child, but with oodles of sex appeal, all over again, pulling out her salad spinner, steaming asparagus and baking cherry clafoutis.

The dark, unyielding man with the heart of stone would succumb. And all would be well.

As it happened, I had a pretty similar experience, sans the drama, of course. You see, my circumstances had changed and I had, for a spell, abandoned my enthusiasm for home cooking.

If I had to entertain, I took people out to the best restaurants. I was a food critic, after all, and knew exactly what would please whom. Cooking just seemed like it wasn't worth the effort.

At which point I met someone who provoked me to snap out of my ennui. I responded by deciding to cook dinner. I could have picked any one of two dozen fail-proof dishes from my repertoire, but I chose this one.

I happen to have the knack of telling from even a few interactions, what food someone enjoys and what they abhor.

I remember eating habits better than I do birthdays. Here was a rice eater and someone who relished seafood. What better than an impressive, elegant prawn biryani.

While the prawn biryani 'finished' under its foil tent in my oven, I changed the cushion covers, filled vases with bunches of gerbera and lit scented candles.

But I think it was only the blissful balance of fragrant rice and perfectly spiced prawns that was remembered from the night. Which is as it should be.

Prawn Biryani

- 1½ cups jeera or Basmati rice, washed and drained
- A tbsp whole garam masala (cardamom, cloves, cinnamon)
- 1 tsp peppercorns
- 1 tsp salt
- 400 gm prawns
- 2 large onions
- 3 large ripe tomatoes
- ½ inch ginger
- 4 green chillies
- 3 tbsp oil
- 1 tsp cumin powder
- 2 tbsp grated coconut
- ½ cup yogurt
- 1 cup coconut milk

First, prepare the rice. Bring 4 cups water to boil in a large pot and put in the whole garam masala and the peppercorns. Let the water simmer away for about half an hour so it is imbued with the spices. Put in the salt and the rice. Let it cook for 8-10 minutes. It should be just tender. Drain the rice. If you are not used to this, simply place a large colander or stainless steel sieve over a large pan and empty the rice and water into it. Once the water has drained away, set the rice aside.

Now, proceed with the prawn masala. Peel, devein, wash the prawns and pat dry. Slice the onion into thin slices. Peel and chop the tomatoes. Grind the ginger and green chillies with a little water. Heat the oil and fry the onion slices a little at a time till brown and crisp. Drain on absorbent paper. Set aside.

In the same oil, put in the green chilli-ginger paste and then the cumin powder. Sauté for a couple of minutes and add the tomatoes. Sauté till the tomatoes are pulpy and the oil separates from the masala. Add the grated coconut and the yogurt, lightly whipped, a little at a time, till it is all incorporated. Add the prawns, add salt to taste and add the coconut milk. Bring to a boil and take off the heat.

To assemble the biryani, spread the prawn masala in an even layer in an oven-proof glass dish. Spread the rice on top and sprinkle over with the fried onions. Cover the dish with foil and bake in an oven at 200°C/400°F/Gas Mark 6 for half an hour.

Alternatively, cook the prawn biryani in the pressure cooker. Spread the prawn masala in a pressure cooker, put the rice on top, sprinkle with the onions and pressure-cook over a low heat for 10 minutes. Serve hot with a raita. Capsicum and pumpkin raita pair especially well with this.

Serves 2-3

60 Prawn Pulao in a Jiffy

If the Prawn Biryani (page 101) is all elegance, requiring a great deal of prepping, then this dish is a quick fix and still very good.

I made it thanks to a friend who is steady, grounded and unflappable and purveys practical wisdom without any attempt to impress. He is also an expert on seafood and has access to some superlative stuff.

I am occasionally the beneficiary of his largesse and get good stocks of super fresh prawns. When I have to cook for a crowd in a hurry, I throw this dish together.

It never fails to please. A big bunch of friends with hearty appetites and some very cold beer is all that it takes to turn this simple effort into a hit meal.

Quick Prawn Pulao

1½ cups fine rice
2 tbsp oil
1 onion, thinly sliced
½ inch ginger, finely chopped
A handful of fresh coriander, chopped
2 ripe tomatoes, chopped
Salt to taste
1 tbsp biryani masala (any brand)
A pinch of turmeric powder
300 gm prawns, shelled and deveined
1 cup thin coconut milk

Wash and soak the rice for about half an hour.

Heat the oil in a pressure cooker; add the onion and ginger and the chopped coriander. Sauté on a low heat till the onion begin to brown.

Add the tomatoes and the salt and cook till the tomatoes are pulpy. Add the biryani masala and the turmeric powder; sauté and add the rice, well drained, and the prawns.

Stir and pour in the coconut milk and enough hot water to come up to about 2 inches above the rice. Close and cook for about 10 minutes. Serve with a raita.

Serves 2-3

To Make a Quick Pumpkin Raita

Take a cupful of pumpkin, peeled and cut into small dice. Boil in salted water till tender. They cook really fast. Drain and cool. Grind a green chilli and half a teaspoon of mustard seeds to a fine paste. Add the green chilli-mustard seeds paste to a cup of salted yogurt. Add a pinch of sugar and stir in the cooked pumpkin.

61 The Things You Can Do with Potatoes!

Because I cook to relax and beat stress, I don't choose overly challenging recipes or complex dishes. But once in a while when I love a dish so much, I am tempted to attempt even a tough one. When I tasted my first gnocchi in Florence it didn't seem like too hard a thing to cook.

But then I went through scores of recipes (I'm a bit wary of ones on the net) including my signed copy of Antonio Carluccio's *Vegetables* and the thing I realised is that everyone tells you how tricky gnocchi are. There were scare stories of them disintegrating in the water or, worse, turning out all hard and chewy instead of the fluffy little pillows they are meant to be.

Never mind, I thought and set out to make potato gnocchi one lazy Sunday evening with my niece who stays with me helping me along with her encouragement. She's a pasta fiend and was only too happy to egg me on.

I have to say I began with trepidation and then what joy it was to see the little ridged mouthfuls bob to the surface, all creamy and fluffy just as they should be. And let me assure you, there's nothing to be scared or nervous about.

There is one thing you should pay attention to though – and that is to use a very light hand with the potatoes and the dough.

Potato Gnocchi

500 gm new potatoes	1 egg yolk, beaten
100 gm refined flour	Salt to taste

Boil the potatoes till tender, peel while still hot and put through a mill. You may use a potato masher, but the idea is to make them smooth and fluffy without overworking.

Add the flour and the egg yolk and knead lightly. The dough should hold together. Roll into logs about one-inch in diameter and cut into half each thick discs.

Pick up each, press your thumb into one side and press down with a fork on the other to create ridges.

Make all the gnocchis this way. Bring a large pot of salted water to the boil and put in the gnocchi in two batches. They will be done in 3-4 minutes and will bob to the surface.

Lift out with a perforated spoon and keep warm. Once both batches are done serve tossed in tomato sauce or pesto.

They are excellent with a drizzle of butter as well. I had a few left over from my dinner and the next morning I had them gratinated with a sprinkling of cheese. Delightful!

Serves 2-3

62 Baked Mustard Chicken

Which foodie doesn't love the food shows on TV? I can spend hours entranced by Anthony Bourdain's adventures in strange places and with even stranger food, watch re-runs of a tipsy Keith Floyd and even the prim Madhur Jaffrey.

Food and travel pieces are the best. But cookery shows can be captivating, too. My favourites from a long time ago are Delia Smith and does anyone remember Yan, from Yan Can Cook?

Among the current crop I find Kylie Kwong's take on Chinese food most refreshing and I did make her fried eggs drizzled with sesame oil which turned out wonderful.

But for sheer oomph quotient you cannot look beyond Nigella Lawson. I love especially her descriptions – a snowfall of crushed meringues and peaches blushing in their syrup while they poach.

Still, you don't normally cook from TV shows, do you? This recipe for a well-seasoned baked chicken by Nigella Lawson is an exception. I like it especially because it's a dish that can be prepared ahead and it doesn't take all that much prepping either. And when you want dinner all you have to do is pop it in the oven and toss up a salad or steam some veggies.

Lemon and Mustard Chicken

1 whole (approx. 1.5 kg) chicken with skin, cut into 6 or 8 serving pieces

1 lemon

1 tsp English mustard, or Dijon, if you like

8 garlic cloves

1 large onion, cut into thick wedges

1 tsp black pepper powder

2 tbsp olive oil

A few good splashes of Worcestershire sauce

A pinch of sage leaves, or other herbs

Salt to taste

Clean and pat dry the chicken. Put it in a large bowl, squeeze in the lemon and add all the other ingredients. Add salt to taste.

Cover and marinate for 10 hours or more.

To cook, place in a roasting tin and bake for about 40 minutes at 180°C/350°F/Gas Mark 4.

Increase the temperature to 220°C/425°F/Gas Mark 7 towards the end of the cooking time to brown the chicken.

Lift out, pour the juices over and serve with roast potatoes, steamed veggies or grilled spring onions, which are delightful accompaniment.

You can add some good pork sausages to this bake if you want to stretch it further.

Serves 4

63 All the Dals Together

I am a dosa fan, anytime, anywhere. As long as it's properly fermented, doesn't have soda bicarbonate or refined flour added to the batter and is made thin and crisp.

And while rice and black gram dosa are everyday tiffin, the adai dosa is special. This dosa made with a combination of pulses and rice needs no fermenting, is packed with nutrition and is delicious, eaten hot and crisp with a good coconut chutney or just white butter.

Adai and avial make a good combo, too. You can vary the proportions, it doesn't change things too much.

You can also add grated coconut or coconut chips, coriander leaves, finely chopped cabbage. And if you can find drumstick leaves, a few tender ones add a nice twist.

Adai

1 cup rice	A pinch of asafoetida
¼ cup skinless split black gram	2 tbsp grated coconut
¼ cup split pigeon peas	2 sprigs curry leaves
¼ cup split Bengal gram	Oil or ghee for shallow-frying
2-3 red chillies	Chutney or butter, as required
Salt to taste	

Soak the pulses and rice together for about 10 hours.

Grind them with a little water, adding the red chillies, salt and asafoetida. Pour the batter into a bowl, add the coconut and the curry leaves. Stir well.

Heat a seasoned dosa tawa and pour the batter in and spread into a thin dosa. Drizzle with ghee or oil and cook till golden brown underneath.

Lift out and serve with chutney or butter. You may turn over the adai if you wish.

Makes about 10 adai

How to Season a Dosa Tawa

A well-seasoned tawa is essential to efficient dosa-making. Heating the tawa to the right temperature is important.

If you sprinkle some water, it should sizzle and evaporate; that's the right amount of heat. If your dosa sticks, try rubbing the tawa with a cut onion.

64 Stuff That!

There's something of a culinary adventure about putting one good thing into another. I'm talking stuffed vegetables here. Think of good ol' capsicum stuffed with aloo masala, aubergines filled and baked to make imam bayildi and tomatoes packed with rice or cheese or meat.

Zucchini filled with rice and mince and simmered in tomato sauce is a middle eastern classic and Italian chefs do wonders by encasing ricotta cheese in squash or pumpkin flowers and then deep-frying them.

Sri Lankan food, which I so adore, has an interesting take on stuffed capsicums. There they use the long, light green chillies (used for chilli bajji here) and simmer it in a fragrant gravy. It's simply delicious.

They almost always use a bit of Maldive fish to perk things up there, but the vegetarian version is just as good.

Stuffed Capsicum Curry

6 slender, long capsicums	1 tsp coriander powder
3 tbsp oil	1 tsp cumin powder
2 small onions, chopped	Salt to taste
2 tsp ginger-garlic paste	A pinch of turmeric powder
250 gm potatoes, boiled	½ cup thick coconut milk
2 tsp chilli powder	

Wash the capsicum and make a slit lengthways without cutting through. Scoop out as many seeds as you can and set aside.

For the filling, heat 1 tablespoon oil in a pan, put in half the onions, sauté till onions begin to brown. Add half the ginger-garlic paste.

Peel and roughly mash the potatoes and add to the onions, along with half of all the spice powders. Add salt to taste.

Take off the heat. Using a small spoon stuff the potato masala into the capsicums.

To cook the capsicums, heat the remaining oil, add the remaining onion and ginger-garlic paste and sauté.

Place the capsicums carefully in the pan, sprinkle with salt and cook, taking care not to break the capsicums. When half done, add the remaining spice powders, turmeric powder and the coconut milk. Let it simmer till the capsicums are tender and the gravy is thick and coats the capsicums.

Serves 3-4

65 Rice, the Italian Way

The first time I ate risotto was at the Italia at The Park, and it was cooked by none other than the famous Antonio Carluccio. Porcini, if I remember right, and perfectly done it was.

Good Italian restaurants will tell you it takes 20 minutes to make risotto, the master chef enlightened me. No pre-cooked and microwaved risotto there – only a la minute. The risotto is a dish that will not be rushed and is good to make when you have to feed close friends who don't mind hanging about your kitchen. This is because the risotto needs a fair amount of attention, but you can sip on wine and chat away while it's cooking.

Risotto rice is now available in most speciality food stores here and that is the kind you must use to achieve the right texture. A good stock is also key. It is great if you can make your own chicken or seafood stock. But, at a pinch, stock cubes work just fine.

My recipe is for a vegetarian risotto, but feel free to experiment, using porcini mushrooms, chicken, prawns or a green mix of tender spinach, asparagus and herbs.

Leek and Mushroom Risotto

2 cups Arborio rice
3 plump leeks
250 gm mushrooms
2 tbsp olive oil
4 garlic cloves
Salt to taste
1 onion, finely chopped
10 cups vegetable stock
½ cup white wine (optional)
Pepper to taste
50 gm grated Parmesan or other sharp cheese
10 gm butter
2 tbsp fresh parsley, chopped

First, prepare the vegetables. Wash the leeks, getting rid of all grit and trim off the green tops. Chop roughly.

Wipe the mushrooms and slice. Heat 1 tablespoon olive oil in a thick-bottomed pan and put in the garlic.

Add the leeks and the mushrooms, a pinch of salt and sauté. When the veggies wilt, lift out and set aside.

In the same pan, heat the remaining oil and add the chopped onion. Fry till all the raw flavour disappears. Add the rice. Meanwhile put the stock to heat.

Sauté the rice till all the grains are coated with the oil and pour in the wine if using. Let it all get absorbed. Start adding the stock, a ladleful at a time.

Let it get absorbed before adding the next ladle. When the rice is three-fourth done add the cooked leek and mushroom, the pepper and continue with the rest of the stock. Your rice should be cooked through, but not mushy.

There must be some broth clinging to the grains. Add the cheese, butter and parsley and mix. Allow to rest for a minute and serve.

Serves 4

66 Kebabs at Home

I do love a good chicken kebab, but I do think way too much is made of it. While some people go on about the murgh tikka or the reshmi kebab at this restaurant or the other, I like making my own kebabs at home.

Chicken kebabs aren't all that hard to perfect. It's merely a matter of marinating in the right blend of spices and grilling it right.

Use a mix of thigh and breast meat for the best flavour. Yogurt makes the best marinade base. Then just play around with your spices and condiments.

Ginger-garlic and green chilli paste, red chilli powder, dhania and jeera, cream and a sprinkle of saffron are all combinations you can attempt. But my favourite kebab to make at home is a good shammi.

I've eaten the best Hyderabadi-style at the home of Saad bin Jung. Mine isn't bad either.

Shammi Kebab

- 500 gm minced mutton
- 100 gm split Bengal gram, washed
- 1 inch ginger, scraped and chopped
- Salt to taste
- 2 dried red chillies
- 1 tbsp mixed whole spices (cardamom, clove, mace, and 1 inch cinnamon)
- 1 tsp peppercorns
- 2 eggs, lightly beaten
- 4 tbsp chopped fresh coriander
- Oil for basting

Put the mutton, the Bengal gram, ginger, salt, red chillies, the mixed whole spices and peppercorns in a pressure cooker.

Pressure-cook for 10 minutes (three whistles). You will not need to add water, as the mutton will give off enough water.

Once cooked, sauté further to remove the moisture and the mutton is dry. Allow to cool and process the mixture in a blender to make a smooth paste.

Transfer to a bowl and mix in the eggs. Do not worry if it seems runny.

Add the chopped coriander and marinate in the refrigerator for an hour. Shape into flat cutlets and shallow-fry till deep brown on both sides.

Serve with onion rings and lime wedges. If you have the patience and want something more elaborate, fill the kebabs with a mixture of hung yogurt, mint and green chillies, close to seal and proceed to shallow-fry them.

Makes about 12

To Make Onion Rings

Peel and slice the onion rings as thin as possible. Place in iced water for 30 minutes. Lift out and pat dry. Serve drizzled with lime juice alongside kebabs.

67 Snack on Shrimp

As I mentioned before, I have a friend who cultivates prawns for a living. And of excellent quality they are, too.

He's also a serious foodie and our conversations are often just raves about the food we've enjoyed: the things we ate as children, the stuff our mothers cook or great food memories from nondescript eateries.

One of the dishes he mentioned which set my mouth-watering was the prawn pakore made in his home and how platefuls would vanish. I didn't get the exact recipe, but I attempted something and it came out real nice.

Prawn Pakora

500 gm prawns	1 tsp ginger-green chilli paste
1 cup bajji-bonda mix	Salt to taste
½ tsp red chilli powder	Oil for deep-frying

Shell and devein the prawns. You may keep the tails on if you like.

Place the prawns in a bowl, put in the bajji-bonda mix, the chilli powder, ginger-green chilli paste and salt.

Sprinkle in about half a cup of water till the prawns are well coated with the batter. Drop tablespoonfuls of the prawn mixture into the hot oil and deep-fry till golden brown.

Drain on absorbent paper and serve hot.

Serves 3-4 as a snack

68-69 Two Kinds of Mango Curry

I don't much care for savoury foods that are also sweet, but mango dishes must be an exception. I do love the harmony between sour and sweet that makes you want to keep eating more.

My favourite mango curries are these two. One is made from unripe green mango, the other from fully ripe fruit. Both can accompany meals of rice or paratha and curry, but I like to eat the unripe green mango pachadi just like that.

These are two dishes that make the mango season even better.

Unripe Mango Pachadi

2 large (approx. 250 gm each) unripe green mangoes
1 tbsp oil
½ tsp mustard seeds
3 dried red chillies, broken into bits
A handful of shallots, peeled and chopped roughly
Salt to taste
Sugar to taste
A sprig of curry leaves

Peel and cut the mango into large chunks. Pressure-cook with a little water for about five minutes (one whistle). Heat the oil in a karhai; add the mustard seeds and the red chillies.

Add the chopped shallots and sauté till they begin to brown. Add the cooked mangoes and mash lightly. Adjust salt and sugar. Add the curry leaves.

Serve at room temperature.

Serves 4

Sweet Mango Pachadi

1 (approx. 250 gm) juicy, ripe mango
1 tsp oil
½ tsp mustard seeds
½ inch ginger, finely chopped
1 red chilli, broken into bits
1 green chilli, chopped
A sprig of curry leaves
A pinch of turmeric powder
Salt to taste
1 cup yogurt, beaten

Peel and cut the mango into cubes.

Heat the oil; add the mustard, the ginger and the chilli. Add the curry leaves and the turmeric powder. Add the mango and salt and sauté for a minute.

Stir in the yogurt and remove from the heat immediately. This tastes very nice with chapati or paratha.

Serves 2

70 Eat Hot or Cold

Fish cakes are an excellent thing – both snack and meal. Eaten straight off the pan with a salad and some bread they can make a light lunch or dinner.

Cold, they are fab for lunch boxes and also for picnics. This recipe is inspired by one in Antonio Carluccio's *Vegetables* where it is, interestingly, listed under recipes for potatoes. Use canned salmon if you can find it. Else, canned tuna works just fine.

Fish Cakes

- 1 small can (400 gm) salmon or tuna
- 400 gm potato
- Salt to taste
- 1 tbsp chopped parsley
- 1 tbsp capers, chopped
- Juice and zest of half a lime
- Freshly ground pepper to taste
- 1 egg, beaten
- 2 cups breadcrumbs
- Oil for deep-frying

Peel and cut the potatoes into chunks and cook in salted water till tender. Drain and mash roughly. Drain the brine or oil from the salmon and flake into thc potatoes.

Add the parsley, capers, lemon zest and juice and salt and pepper powder to taste. Add the egg and mix everything together.

Shape into cakes, roll in the breadcrumbs and deep-fry in oil till golden brown. Serve warm or cold.

Makes 10 cakes

71 Trouble-free Finger Food

I do love entertaining at home. I enjoy good company as much as I do cooking. So what can be better than asking a bunch of friends over to a few rounds of drinks and a special dinner afterwards. It doesn't have to be elaborate – just thought out well and cooked with care. And these days I increasingly prefer kicking back at home to getting dressed up to go to a restaurant.

And if you plan and prepare in advance you can have as good a time as your guests. It also comes from evolving – giving up the desire to wow one's friends and focussing instead on ensuring that everyone has an easy, relaxed time. So, if a friend suggests we go do a whisky tasting at some spiffy bar, I'm rather more likely to say that we spend the money on a good bottle and spend the evening at home, eating something from my kitchen.

If my guests are drinking I always like to serve something homemade for nibbles. It doesn't have to be elegant or fussy, just something besides chips or tortilla chips from a packet. One thing that always hits the spot are these somewhat posh egg-mayo on toast. They are the perfect pre-dinner nibble and I don't know anyone who doesn't like them.

Posh Eggs in Mayo on Toast

Focaccia, if you can get it or 5 slices bread
4 tbsp butter, softened
3 eggs, boiled
4 tbsp good mayonnaise
1 tsp English mustard
Salt to taste
1 spring onion stalk, finely sliced
Black pepper powder to taste

If you manage to get a good focaccia, cut it into 1½-inch squares. If using regular sliced bread, use a small round cookie cutter and cut 2 or 3 rounds from each slice. Spread the butter on each round.

Toast the focaccia (or bread rounds) in an oven at 200°C/400°F/ Gas Mark 6 for 6 to 8 minutes or till pale brown and crisp. Allow to cool. To make the topping, peel and roughly mash the eggs. Add the mayo and the mustard; adjust the seasoning. Pile small spoonfuls on top of each bread round, top with a spring onion ring, sprinkle with pepper and serve.

Makes about 12 toasts

72 Just the Thing at Midnight

This is for one of my very good friends. He used to drink, I must admit, a tad too much occasionally. And would neglect to eat. He is also one of the most generous souls I know and always ready for a good time. He buys round after round of drinks for everyone in the group and though he scarcely looks at the food, he orders platefuls for everyone else.

But occasionally he would want to eat and it was invariably chilli-cheese toast at his club or even a five-star hotel. I once convinced him to eat my version and this picky eater did quite enjoy it. So, make this for a hungry child or a friend who needs some nourishment at the end of a long night of drinking.

Chilli-Cheese Toast

4 slices good quality bread
1 tbsp butter
1 cup grated cheese
½ tsp English mustard
1 or 2 (if you like it real hot) green chillies, finely chopped

Mix the butter, cheese, mustard and green chillies together. You can add a dash of chilli sauce as well.

Lightly toast the bread in an oven at 200°C/400°F/Gas Mark 6. Remove from the oven and spread the cheese mixture generously on each slice. Return to the oven and bake till the cheese melts and starts bubbling.

Eat hot, but watch that the cheese doesn't burn your mouth.

Serves 2

73 From a Chef's Repertoire

My career as a restaurant critic may have seemed utterly glamorous from the outside, but take it from me, it's not all that it's cut out to be. Yes, of course, you get special treatment, the best table in the house, more prawns in your appetiser and lots of fawning attention. Still, despite the occasional gourmet experience, there's a lot of mediocre food out there and you have to wade through it all. And week after week, at that.

So, for me, the best part of being a restaurant critic was not so much the perks and the privileges, but the occasion to get up close with some of the best cooking talent around. We would begin as professional acquaintances with a measure of mutual respect. But with some chefs and restaurateurs, the first visit to review their restaurants would lead to more meetings and we would move from `what is she going to say about my food' to being two people who shared a love of good food.

Talking food with a knowledgeable chef is such a joy! I can spend hours asking about some ingredient or the other, or discussing the culinary trends of the moment. These are the foodie's non-eating pleasures. And one of the chefs whose company I enjoy is Manu Chandra. With him, I have sat drinking both our favourite rum and cokes and talking for hours – about, what else, food. This, I consider the real reward of being a restaurant critic. Manu has shared many of his fab recipes with me, but the one I find myself turning to most often is for this unadorned fried chicken. It is the perfect snack to serve with drinks.

Pollo Frito

500 gm boneless chicken, cut into ½-inch cubes
2 tsp lemon juice
Salt and pepper to taste
Refined flour for dredging
Oil for deep-frying

Marinate the chicken in the lemon juice, salt and pepper for about 12 hours. When you wish to serve the pollo frito, spread the flour on a sheet of paper and toss the chicken pieces to coat. Deep-fry in hot oil for about six to eight minutes till golden brown. Drain on absorbent paper and serve with a mayonnaise dip, seasoning it with herbs, sauces, chopped capers or olives as you desire.

Serves 2-3 as a snack

74-76 Three Kinds of Mashed Potato

Confession time: I am a fiend for potatoes. They are my favourite vegetable. Well, hello, they are vegetables. And nothing pleases me more than mashed potatoes. I am known to throw decorum aside and ask chefs serving steak with all manner of chic sides to make it mashed potatoes, please, and lots of it.

Even as a child my sick-bed favourite was mashed potatoes. And because I love mashed potatoes so very much I have spent a fair amount of time getting them just right. So, I assure you this recipe will make you a bowl of mashed potatoes you can eat just like that.

Then there's podimaas which really is a South Indian mashed potato, wouldn't you say? Try it with some sambar rice.

Aloo bhat or Bengali-style mashed potatoes served with rice I discovered thanks to our holidays in Kolkata. It is starch on starch and excellent.

Fab Mashed Potatoes

500 gm potatoes	1 cup milk
50 gm butter	Salt and pepper to taste

Make sure you use new potatoes which have a floury texture. Peel and cut the potatoes into large chunks. Place in a large pot of water and bring to the boil. Allow the potatoes to cook till completely tender. Test with a knife.

Drain and return the pan to the heat to dry off any excess moisture.

While still hot, mash with a fork, add the butter and beat in as much milk as you like. Season with salt and pepper. Eat and be comforted.

Note: Mashed potatoes are best made from just cooked potatoes and eaten warm.

Serves 2-3 mashed potato lovers

Podimaas

500 gm potatoes	½ inch ginger chopped
1 tbsp oil	2 green chillies, chopped
½ tsp mustard seeds	1 sprig curry leaves
½ tsp skinless split black gram	Salt to taste
A pinch of asafoetida	2 tbsp grated coconut (optional)

Boil and peel the potatoes. Mash roughly. Heat the oil in a pan, put in all the ingredients except grated coconut and salt and then add the potatoes.

Stir well, adjust seasoning and sprinkle the grated coconut and serve with rice and sambar.

Serves 4

Aloo Bhat

500 gm potatoes	2 green chillies, finely chopped
Salt to taste	3 tbsp mustard oil

Boil and peel the potatoes. Mash while hot and add salt to taste, along with the green chillies. Pour the mustard oil and mix well.

Serve with plain boiled rice. You can introduce more of a mustard zing to the potatoes by adding a little ground mustard.

Serves 2-3

77 Why You Should Buy a Pasta Maker

I met Isabella Allegrini from the Italian winery of the same name for a brief interview. She was a fascinating woman as passionate about food as she was about her Amarone. And, then, as often happens between foodies we began talking endlessly about food and I told her of my interest in Italian cuisine.

Then, unbeknownst to me, she left behind a pasta machine for me to use. Thank you Ms Allegrini. I have had so much fun using it. Hand-rolled pasta is nothing like the dried stuff. It takes no more than a knob of butter to enjoy a bowl of freshly cut and cooked pasta.

And though it does seem daunting to make your own pasta, it's not that hard, really. And you do get better with time and experience. When a pasta maker really comes in handy is for making ravioli. The results are truly rewarding.

Cream Cheese and Spinach Ravioli

For the Ravioli

2 cups refined flour

2 large eggs

For the Filling

2 large bunches (approx. 500 gm) spinach, washed and drained

4 tbsp cream cheese

½ cup cottage cheese

Salt and pepper to taste

For the Sauce

50 gm butter

Fresh herbs, such as sage

Parmesan cheese, as required

To make the pasta, make a mound of the flour, make a well in the centre and pour in the egg a little at a time, drawing everything together to make a smooth dough. Alternatively, use a food processor to knead the dough.

Now pass the dough through the pasta machine, following the instructions. You turn a knob to reduce the thickness of the pasta sheet with each round and end up with a very thin, silken sheet.

To make the filling, blanch the spinach in boiling water till wilted, refresh in cold water, drain and squeeze dry. Chop roughly and process in a blender along with the cream cheese and cottage cheese. Adjust the seasoning.

To make the ravioli, cut the sheet in half. Lay one half on a flat surface and place spoonfuls of filling about two inches apart. Cover with the other sheet and press down around each mound of filling. Cut into squares around each mound of filling.

Bring a large pot of salted water to a boil and add the ravioli gently. They are done when they bob up to the surface. Lift out carefully and set aside.

To make the tossing sauce, melt the butter and add 3-4 tbsp of the water in which the ravioli has been cooked. Put in the herbs and toss the ravioli in this, Serve hot, sprinkled with freshly grated Parmesan cheese.

Serves 2-3

A Super Sauce for Fresh Pasta

For two large portions of fresh pasta, melt 3 tbsp butter, add ½ tsp chopped garlic and whisk in a tsp of good quality mustard such as Dijon. Toss your pasta in this sauce. It is spectacular. You can add herbs to the mustard-butter mixture and enrich your dish with some steamed broccoli as well.

78 A Healthy Chinese Snack

As I said before, I always attempt to put out some interesting snacks with pre-dinner drinks. It just makes the drinking and the conversation that much more pleasurable.

But I have had fussy company who won't eat fried things or nibbles with cheese in them. On those occasions I find myself searching for light, healthy bites which won't look like they came out of a weight loss recipe book.

These steamed morsels are wonderful. I conjured them up from several different recipes and I'm pretty proud of the results.

Chicken Pearls

300 gm boneless chicken	Salt and pepper to taste
2 spring onions	1 egg, lightly beaten
½ tsp minced ginger	½ cup rice, soaked for half an hour
Dash of soy sauce	

Chill the chicken for an hour or so and then mince. It is always better to mince your own chicken than to buy pre-minced.

Chop the spring onion finely and add to the chicken with all the other ingredients except the rice. Mix well and shape into small balls and leave on a greased plate.

Drain the rice and spread on a sheet of paper. Take each chicken ball and roll in the rice to cover completely.

Set these on a greased plate and steam for 10 minutes by which time both the rice and the chicken should be well cooked.

Serve hot with any Oriental-style dipping sauce.

Makes 10 morsels

79 A Make-ahead Meal

This is my fall-back-on-every-time dish when I have a busy day. It can be made up completely and will sit uncomplainingly in the refrigerator until it's time to bake and serve. So whether it's when I'm going to be out all day and need to feed a crowd when I get back, or when I'm going to be so zapped I won't have the energy to whip up dinner, I always make my mac 'n' cheese ahead.

It's very adaptable – you can keep it just plain and cheesy, add mushrooms, shrimp or ham. Top it with tomato slices if you like, or just go for the breadcrumbs alone. Here is my basic recipe, to which I then add whatever ingredients capture my fancy.

Mac 'n' Cheese

- 1 packet (250 gm) macaroni
- 2 tbsp butter
- 4 tbsp refined flour
- 500 ml milk
- 50 gm grated sharp cheese, such as cheddar
- 2 tsp English mustard
- Salt and pepper to taste
- 1 cup breadcrumbs
- Butter, as required

Cook the macaroni according to the instructions on the packet. Set aside. To make the sauce, heat the butter in a thick-bottomed pan. Add the flour and stir and cook without browning.

Pour in the milk, whisking all the time. Do not panic if it lumps a bit at the beginning. The lumps can be whisked away. Now add the cheese, mustard and seasoning. You should have a smooth, custard-like cheese sauce.

Put the cooked macaroni into a baking dish. Pour the sauce over. If you are eating later, cover the dish with a cling film and refrigerate. Before baking, preheat the oven to 180°C/350°F/ Gas Mark 4. Scatter the breadcrumbs on top of the sauce. Dot with the butter and bake till the top is golden brown and crisp.

Serves 2-3

To Make the Breadcrumbs
Run 3-4 slices of slightly stale bread through a blender.

80 All Wrapped Up

Forget the health scares about clogged arteries, I cannot resist the salty, smoky taste of good bacon. What can be better than a couple of rashers fried crisp and an egg, sunny side up, for breakfast on a cold morning? Or some crisp bacon bits in a green salad. Or the salty bite of the stuff in a creamy carbonara.

Bacon is one of those fab foods which can uplift any dish to the next plane. And when it's the centre-piece then it's a sure winner with any bacon fan.

Bacon-wrapped Prunes

12 dried prunes, stoned
6 bacon rashers

Trim and cut each bacon rasher in half. Wrap each prune in a bacon piece, secure neatly with a toothpick.

Grill at 180°C/350°F/Gas Mark 4 for 10 minutes. These make splendid canapés.

Makes 12 bites

81 Chinese at Home

Chinese must be one of my favourite foods while eating out. But, unfortunately, Bangalore's restaurants don't offer fare that quite hits the spot. Greasy Chinese with strong Indian flavours is a no-no for me and that is what most places serve.

In Bangalore, I find the small family-run places do the sort of Chinese which appeals to me far more. A recent discovery has been Kim Lee in Indiranagar introduced to me by a foodie friend. He had promised it would be good ol' Kolkata-style Chinese and it was just that.

Often, when a Chinese food craving strikes, I make something comforting at home. These pan-fried noodles fit the bill.

Pan-fried Noodles

1 packet (250 gm) noodles
4 tbsp oil
1 cup mushrooms, sliced
1 capsicum, cut into strips
1 carrot, sliced
1 head pok choy or Chinese cabbage
4 spring onion stalks, cleaned and cut into lengths
1 cup bean sprouts, tailed
1½ cups stock or
2 stock cubes dissolved in 1½ cups of water
2 tsp cornflour dissolved in half cup water
A dash of soy sauce or fish sauce

Cook the noodles according to the instructions given on the packet. Drain and toss in a tablespoon of oil. Set aside.

Make this dish just as you are about to eat. Heat 2 tablespoon oil in a non-stick frying pan. Put in the noodles and press down to make a sort of flat cake. Let it cook undisturbed on low heat for about ten minutes. The idea is to get a crisp base.

Once done, turn over carefully and brown the other side. You can use a plate to help you along. It's okay if it breaks a bit, just patch things together.

While the noodles are getting crisp, make the vegetable sauce. Heat the remaining oil in a pan, add the vegetables one at a time, stir-fry on a high heat. When they are wilted, add the stock or the stock cube and water. Add the soy sauce and the cornflour mixture. Cook, stirring till the sauce is smooth and translucent. Adjust the seasoning.

To serve, place the noodles in a large platter, pour the vegetables on top and serve hot.You may add some boneless chicken slices or cooked pork to the vegetables. This sauce is also very nice on top of rice cooked in stock.

Serves 2-3

82,83 Two Soups

Our cooking repertoires are often determined by the size of our households. In my parents' homes, earlier in Colombo and then in Madurai, it was always open house and there were a vast number of people to be fed at each meal.

So piles of idli or idiappam would appear for breakfast and dinner and it was always rice and curries for lunch. But now in my little household of two – my niece and I – we eat quite differently.

It's usually oatmeal porridge or toast for breakfast, a packed lunch of pasta or chapati rolls and a hot dinner of noodles, homemade pasta or grills.

Appam, puttu and idiappam breakfasts are for Sundays. Some days we settle for just soup and garlic bread which we eat in front of the TV. These are two of my easy soups and very nourishing they are.

Creamy Broccoli Soup

1 small head (about 300 gm) broccoli	1 onion, thinly sliced
	1 potato, peeled and chopped
2 tbsp butter	2 cups stock or water
2 garlic cloves	Salt and pepper to taste

Separate the broccoli head into small florets. Set aside.

Heat the butter in a thick-bottomed pan and add the garlic and the onion. Sauté lightly.

Add the potato, stir about and add the broccoli. Add the stock and bring to a boil.

Cook till the potatoes are tender. Allow to cool and blend to a smooth purée. Reheat; add salt and pepper to taste.

Serve with a swirl of cream if you like. With some garlic toast this makes for a complete meal.

Serves 2

Egg Drop Soup

2 tsp oil	2 cups stock
2 garlic cloves, chopped	Salt and pepper to taste
1 small carrot, finely chopped	1 egg, beaten lightly with a fork
4 button mushrooms, chopped	1 spring onion stalk, sliced

Heat the oil in a pan. Add the garlic, let it sizzle for a minute and then add the carrot. Sauté briskly; add the mushrooms. Pour in the stock and bring to a boil. Adjust the seasoning.

Now pour the egg in a stream through the tines of a fork into the soup. It will break into small light strands. Turn off the heat, sprinkle the spring onion on top and serve in bowls. You may add a dash of soya sauce or chilli sauce for an extra kick.

Serves 2

84 Bread 'n' Butter Pudding

Food is so much like fashion, changing constantly as it's driven by fads and trends. Think quiche as a party staple. And does anyone do caramel custard anymore? Nah, it's got to be crème brûlée in green tea flavour. You don't want to be caught being unfashionable, right? But then there are also the retro classics that come back with new tastes and greater panache than before.

I have, increasingly, been seeing prawn cocktails, for instance, showing up at elegant affairs. And was also most pleased to see a big warm dish of bread pudding rub shoulders with all the little spoonfuls of quivering, creamy things at a stylish poolside brunch not so long ago.

I confess, I do love bread pudding. Its buttery sweetness takes one back to childhood and comforting foods. Bread `n' butter puddings make a lovely dessert after a not-too-heavy meal and are a good after-school snack as well. You can make these quite luxurious by using brioche, instead of regular white bread, adding candid peel and other exotica or a dash of liqueur. But I usually keep mine simple.

Bread 'n' Butter Pudding

8 slices fresh white bread	½ cup sugar
4 tbsp butter	2 cups whole milk
½ cup raisins	A dash of vanilla or a pinch of grated nutmeg
2 eggs	

Trim the crusts from the bread and butter the slices liberally. Cut into small squares and place in a pie dish.

Sprinkle the raisins. Beat the eggs with the sugar and pour in the milk. Add the vanilla or nutmeg. Strain this mixture into the bread. Dot the surface with the remaining butter.

Bake at 170°C/325°F/Gas Mark 3, until the surface is golden brown and the custard is set. This should take about 30 minutes. Serve warm or cold, with a fruit compote on the side, if you like.

Serves 2-3

85 Little Pots of Luxury

This dish to me is a kitchen triumph. After all, one only ever ate crème brûlée in nice restaurants. The first time I made this dessert was to round off a lavish Sunday lunch with cold meats and homemade pizza, not to mention plenty of wine.

For the crème brûlée I went out and bought little oven-proof dishes for the purpose. That's how I keep adding to my collection

of kitchenware and equipment. It is to serve Khau Swey that I bought the white, old-fashioned soup plates which I now so love.

The little crème brûlée moulds count among my favourite pieces as well. I love them because the dessert turns out so well. I do it two ways. One is to bake the custard till set and then chill it till very firm, top with sugar and place under a hot grill.

The other is to make a stove top custard sauce that's really thick and then chill it and proceed. And if you find real vanilla beans, do use them. Else, essence will do.

Restaurants, I know, use fancy blow torches to get the wafer thin and crisp caramel topping of this dessert. I simply pop my moulds under a very hot grill and it always works. Now you know why I think of it as a small culinary victory....

Crème Brûlée

600 ml heavy cream	1 tsp vanilla essence
4 egg yolks	2 tbsp soft brown sugar
75 gm caster sugar	

Place the cream in a heat-proof bowl and place over a larger pan of simmering water. Let it heat up, but do not let it boil.

Meanwhile, whisk the egg yolks and caster sugar together. When the cream has cooled to being slightly warm, beat it into the egg yolk mixture. Add the vanilla.

Pour into six small ramekin moulds. Set in a baking tin with an inch of water in it.

Bake at 150°C/300°F/Gas Mark 2 for 40 minutes or till the custard is set. Remove and chill well.

Then, sprinkle the top with the brown sugar and place under a hot grill till the sugar has caramelised. Return to the refrigerator and chill for two hours before serving.

Some fruit, such as strawberries or kiwi slices make an attractive decoration for this dessert.

Makes six small moulds

86 An Easy, Impressive Cake

I'm a happy baker. In fact, baking is my stress-buster. So, if you find me pulling out my electric beater out and lining my cake trays, chances are that I've been feeling a little blue. And baking a simple butter cake often provides relief, even if it doesn't solve the problem. It has, I guess, to do with the discipline required in measuring out ingredients, putting them together in a precise fashion, beating, whisking, folding in and then waiting patiently, calmly for the results to emerge from the oven. Share what you've made, spreading some sweet generosity around, and the world sure seems a better place. Which is also why I so love baking birthday cakes for friends, family and colleagues.

It takes away the trouble of thinking up gifting options, too, for who doesn't appreciate a homemade birthday cake! My nieces and nephews are all chocolate fiends, so I invariable make any one of half a dozen kinds of chocolate cake for them. But for those who are willing to think beyond chocolate, I would make my lemon drizzle cake. It's moist and luscious without being too rich.

Lemon Drizzle Cake

175 gm refined flour
1 tsp baking powder
125 gm butter + for greasing
175 gm caster sugar
2 eggs, beaten
2 lemons or limes
50 gm coarse sugar

Preheat the oven to 180°C/350°F/Gas Mark 4.

Grease with butter and line an 8-inch square cake tin. Sift the flour with the baking powder. Cream butter and caster sugar until light and fluffy. Add the beaten eggs gradually, beating in 1 tbsp flour after each addition. Add the grated rind of one lemon. Squeeze in its juice. Mix well. Bake for 25 minutes.

Peel the zest of the other lemon. Mix the zest with half the granular sugar. Set aside. Squeeze the juice of the lemon into a pan and add the remaining granular sugar. Cook over low heat till you have a thick syrup. Prick the baked cake with a skewer; pour the syrup over it. Scatter with the sugared zest. Cut into squares and serve.

Makes 12 squares

87 Perfectly English

These buttery goodies are thought of as the highpoint of a high tea. For a long time my notion of scones was gathered only from books about English teatime and photographs in the glossy women's magazines of the past.

And then restaurants in Bangalore started putting out high teas – with scones on the menu, naturally. Not all of them are good.

At some brunches, even in five-star hotels, I've eaten nasty hard things. But scones are a breeze to bake. And so quick, too.

Serve them when you have unexpected guests over at teatime and lap up the applause.

Easy Scones

225 gm refined flour + 1 tbsp for dusting
1 tsp baking powder
A pinch of salt
40 gm butter, cubed
15 gm caster sugar
150 ml milk

Preheat the oven to 220°C/425°F/Gas Mark 7. Sift the flour, baking powder and salt into a large bowl. Rub in butter until the mixture resembles breadcrumbs.

Stir in the sugar. Add enough milk for a soft dough. Knead lightly till smooth. Roll into ¾-inch thick disc and cut into 2-inch rounds.

Draw the trimmings together, roll again and cut out more circles.

Place the scones, a little distance apart, on a lightly greased baking sheet. Brush the tops with milk, dust with flour. Bake for 12-15 minutes. These are best eaten warm.

Split and spread with butter or cream and jam. Scrumptious!

Makes 8 scones

88 One Good Thing on Top of Another

I like to eat healthy, sure. But there are times when I crave unctuous, gooey, sweet delights. And I'm completely against trying to make these into health foods by putting oatmeal into cupcakes, replacing butter with yogurt and adding honey instead of sugar in a cookie.

Indulge, when you must, but exercise moderation is my key to handling sweet cravings, or any other deep culinary desire for that matter.

I found the recipe for these caramel slices, also referred to as millionaire's shortbread, in a second hand book titled *Comfort Food*. It's a luscious combination of molten caramel on a buttery, crumbly crust. A veneer of dark chocolate finishes the slice. The kids in my family love these confections, as do the grown-ups.

Caramel Slice

For the Base and Topping	For the Caramel
115 gm butter + for greasing	175 gm butter
175 gm refined flour	115 gm sugar
55 gm golden caster sugar	3 tbsp golden syrup
200 gm plain chocolate	400 gm condensed milk

Preheat the oven to 180°C/350°F/Gas Mark 4. Grease a 9-inch cake tin. Run the butter, flour and sugar briefly though a food processor. Press into the tin and bake for 20 minutes.

For the caramel, place all ingredients in a thick-bottomed pan and stir on a low heat for 8 minutes. You should have a thick mixture that pulls away from the pan.

Pour on top of crust. Chill for two hours. Melt the chocolate. Leave to cool a bit then spread over the caramel. Chill. Cut into slices and serve.

Makes 16 slices

89 A Cupful of Joy

Look at what happened to the everyday cupcake! From a kiddy party staple it's gone all chic and trendy. Cupcakes are photographed and written about and cupcake-making has become a whole new industry.

I've been hearing of women with excellent corporate careers throwing it all up to pursue their passion for making cupcakes. Talk about food fads! As for me, I made cupcakes when I began baking as a child, and I had no idea they were going to become the gourmet rage they are at present.

They were basic butter cakes, maybe with a swirl of butter icing on the surface or a dollop of jam in the centre to give them an added richness. But now I've got on the bandwagon, too, and I love `tarting' up my cupcakes with pastel coloured glazes and icing and all manner of fancy flourishes.

I love doing an all butter cupcake, topping it with a smooth layer of lemon icing and then crowning it with a delicate rosebud of pink sugar. I often make these as surprise gifts for friends – as get well gestures, to say sorry when I've goofed up or simply to tell someone I thought of them. It almost always works.

Easy Cupcakes

175 gm refined flour	3 large eggs
1 level tsp baking powder	1 tsp vanilla
175 gm unsalted butter	18 paper cups
175 gm caster sugar (or run regular sugar through a mixer)	

Line a muffin tray with paper cups.

Preheat the oven to 170°C/325°F/Gas Mark 3. Sift the flour with the baking powder.

Ensure the butter is at room temperature and soft. Place in a large bowl, add the sugar and beat till pale and fluffy.

Add the eggs one at a time, ensuring each is well incorporated before adding the next. Put in the vanilla and add the flour.

You may continue to mix with your electric beater, but do not overbeat. Once the flour is mixed in, put a large tablespoon of batter into each cup. Do not fret if the tops aren't level, they will smooth out in the baking.

Bake for about 15 minutes until risen and golden on the top. Serve as is, or top with lemon glacé or butter-cream and decorations.

Makes 16 slices

For the Lemon Glacé

1 cup icing sugar, sifted

Juice of 1 large lemon

Pour the lemon juice into the icing sugar and mix well. You should have a fairly thin icing. Pour spoonfuls on the top of each cake; it will spread and form a glaze. Top with hundreds and thousands, chocolate vermicelli or sugar roses.

How to Make Sugar Roses

Sift half a cup of icing sugar into a bowl. Add a pinch of gelatin. Pour in enough liquid glucose to knead into a smooth dough. Knead well and add pink colour. Pinch off bits and shape roughly into heart shapes. Fold one to shape into a roll for the centre of the rose. Arrange the other heart shaped petals around to form a rose and pinch together at the base.

90 Lemon Squares

I collect recipe books with a passion, stocking them up the way other women collect expensive bags or accessories. Some of them are prized possessions, the Prada bags of my bookshelf. These are the ones signed by chefs and the expensive ones, like my *Culinaria* editions. But not all cost thousands of rupees.

Many years ago on the pavements near Flora Fountain in Bombay I bought for Rs 50 a wonderful hardbound book titled *Hundred Glories of French Cooking* – and what a glorious read it is! I love stylishly written books – with MFK Fisher topping the list. Jeffrey Steingarten is splendid, too, and Anthony Bourdain makes even recipe books bristle with attitude.

I'm not terribly discerning when it comes to buying food books though. Most anything will do. If it catches my eye and I have the money, I'll buy. Which is how I landed up with useless publications like *Just Three Ingredients*.

These, in a particular recipe, would be 1 can chicken soup, 1 tin mushrooms and 1 readymade piecrust-to make a chicken pie, in case you were wondering. But in second hand book stores and on pavements I have found some gems.

One was called *A Little Book of Baking*. I don't recall by whom. And it's gone into that dark place where lent books that are never returned go. But I have this recipe which makes a wonderful bake and here it is:

Lemon Squares

175 gm + 2 tbsp refined flour	A pinch of salt
125 gm butter + for greasing	2 medium eggs
50 gm granulated sugar	Juice and rind of 2 lemons
200 gm caster sugar	Icing sugar for dusting
½ tsp baking powder	

Preheat the oven to 170°C/325°F/Gas Mark 3.

Grease with butter and line an 8-inch square tin. Rub together 175 gram flour and butter. Stir in granulated sugar and mix well.

Turn into the tin and bake for 20 minutes. Beat together caster sugar, 2 tablespoons refined flour, baking powder, salt, eggs, lemon juice and rind till smooth.

Pour over the base. Bake for another 20 minutes till nearly set. Allow to cool and dust with icing sugar.

Cut into slices and serve or send out as a gift for someone who likes zesty things.

Makes 16 slices

91 My Fave Chocolate Cake

Every ardent baker has a line-up of chocolate cake recipes in her collection – from the basic cocoa powder in buttercake mix to exotic, deep, dark sinful things.

I have been through the gamut, even testing a batter with copious amounts of yogurt in it. But my current favourite is the mocha cake from the *Tassajara Cookbook*, a stained copy of which I found in a second-hand bookstore. It caught my attention because I'd been reading about Edward Espé Brown, the chef and Zen Buddhist priest.

The story of his raisin meditation has remained with me. Edward would guide his students on seeing, sensing, tasting food by asking them to hold a few raisins in their palms and do no more than feel them, then put them in their mouth and still just feel their sensation without chewing or swallowing.

The gratification of taste would only come at the end of this long, patient process. He emphasises the need to be mindful, while cooking and eating. Try it, it's an interesting experiment.

Tassajara is, in fact, a Zen centre in California and their cookbook is an interesting mix of tofu dishes, nut loaves and bakes. I tried the mocha cake and it turns out beautiful. Just make sure you use the best quality chocolate you can find.

Mocha Cake

120 gm dark chocolate
½ cup butter + for greasing
1 cup coffee
2 cups flour
2 cups sugar
¼ tsp salt
1½ tsp soda bicarbonate
1 cup yogurt
1 tsp vanilla
2 eggs, beaten
Cocoa, for dusting

For the Frosting

175 gm chocolate
½ cup coffee
100 gm butter

Melt the chocolate, butter and coffee over a pan of simmering water. Sift the flour with sugar, salt, soda bicarbonate.

Pour the chocolate mixture into the dry ingredients.

Add the yogurt, vanilla and mix in the eggs. Grease two 8-inch tins with the butter. Dust with cocoa. Pour in the batter. Bake for 30 minutes.

For the frosting, warm the chocolate and coffee over a pan of hot water. Beat in the butter gradually. The mixture will thicken as it cools. Spread over the top and sides of the cake.

Makes 12 slices

92 Fruit and Chocolate

When I was working full-time for a newspaper I headed a small team of bright, young things. We made a big deal of everyone's birthdays and passed the hat around for a cash gift. I would always chip in with a cake. And this one used to go down very well.

Chocolate-Orange Marble Cake

125 gm butter + for greasing
125 gm refined flour
1 tsp baking powder
125 gm caster sugar
Zest of 1 orange
2 eggs
2 tbsp orange juice
50 gm dark chocolate
1 tbsp cocoa powder

For the Topping

1 tsp cocoa powder
1 tbsp icing sugar

Preheat the oven to 180°C/350°F/Gas Mark 4. Grease with butter and line a 500 gram loaf tin or cake tin.

Sift the flour with the baking powder. Cream together the butter, sugar orange zest. Gradually add eggs. Sift in flour and pour in the orange juice. Fold in gently.

Divide the batter into two equal portions. Melt the chocolate over a pan of simmering water. Add the melted chocolate and cocoa to one half and mix well.

Drop alternate blobs of the orange and chocolate batter into the baking tin. Drag a knife through the batter to create a ripple effect. Bake for 35 minutes.

Dust with cocoa and icing sugar before cutting and serving.

Makes 12 slices

93 Start Baking with Yeast

Baking is one of the most gratifying things you can do in your kitchen. You stir, you beat, you knead, you pop it into the oven and wait, hoping for the best. No matter how many times I've baked the same thing, there is always that little measure of uncertainty – perhaps it's the amount of leavening or the humidity. And what can be more satisfying than seeing that perfect muffin emerge from the oven or smelling the sweet waft from freshly-baked brownies.

But the joy of baking with yeast is of another kind altogether. There is all that therapeutic kneading, to begin with and then watching the miracle of rising dough. To see a crusty, gold brown loaf or bun come out of the oven is the baker's very special reward. When I go home to visit my sister and family I almost always make a large batch of raisin buns. The whole family loves them.

Raisin Buns

25 gm butter + for greasing
2 tbsp caster sugar
120 ml milk + 1 tbsp for glazing
225 gm refined flour
½ tsp salt
1 tsp instant dried yeast
1 egg, beaten
½ cup raisins, cleaned and dried

Gently heat the butter, sugar and milk in a pan. Place the flour, salt and yeast in a large pan. Make a well in the middle of the flour. Reserve 1 tbsp of the beaten egg and pour the rest into the well along with the lukewarm milk mixture. Add the raisins and mix to form a soft dough. Knead for 10 minutes.

Cover with a damp cloth and leave to rise in a warm place for about an hour. Knock back the dough, shape into golf ball-sized balls and place on a lightly greased baking tray. Allow to rise again till double in size. Mix together 1 tablespoon milk and the reserved egg and brush the top of the buns with the mixture.

Place in an oven preheated to 200°C/400°F/Gas Mark 6 and bake for about 20 minutes.

Makes about 12 buns

94 Sinful and So Good

Every keen baker attempts brownies at some point. And early attempts invariably end in too dry or crumbly results.

Brownie-making is, in fact, something that you can spend a long time perfecting, experimenting with ways to make your goodies richer and more gooey as you go along.

Some people add a dash of coffee liqueur, others use only dark chocolate, no cocoa. There are ways and ways. Here is my recipe, tweaked and tested.

Chocolate Brownies

- 100 gm butter + for greasing
- 100 gm chocolate
- 200 gm soft sugar
- 2 eggs, beaten
- 140 gm flour
- ¼ tsp baking powder
- A pinch of salt
- 1 tsp vanilla
- ½ cup chopped walnuts (optional)

Preheat the oven to 180°C/350°F/Gas Mark 4.

Grease with butter and line an 8-inch tin. Melt the chocolate and butter over a pan of simmering water. Remove from the heat and add the sugar. Beat in the eggs.

Sift the flour with the baking powder and salt and add to the chocolate mixture. Add the vanilla.

Stir in the walnuts if using. Pour into the prepared tin and bake for 25 minutes. Be careful not to over bake.

When cool, cut into squares and serve or store in an airtight tin.

Makes 16 squares

95 A Warm Dessert for a Cool Evening

I love to keep things simple when I entertain, but dessert, I think is de rigueur – even if it's just fresh fruit, such as oranges sprinkled with sugar and cinnamon or some good quality vanilla ice cream with a splash of Kahlua.

But if you are up to making a simple dessert, a fruit crumble is just perfect. It is best served warm, so have everything assembled and pop in the oven just as your guests start dinner.

Apple Crumble

For the Fruit Base

2 tart green apples
4 tbsp sugar
2 tsp lemon juice
A pinch of cinnamon powder

For the Topping

1 cup refined flour
½ cup butter
½ cup sugar

To Serve

Fresh cream or ice cream

Peel and slice the apples. Place in a baking dish.

Sprinkle over the sugar, lemon juice and cinnamon powder. Toss to mix lightly. Combine the ingredients for the topping, till they resemble breadcrumbs.

Spread the crumble mixture over the fruit. Bake at 180°C/350°F/ Gas Mark 4 for about 20 minutes, by which time the fruit should be soft and the crumble, golden and crisp.

Serve warm with fresh cream or ice cream. For a variation, you could use half pineapple and half apple. Experiment with other fruit as well.

Serves 4

96 Baking for the Weight-Watcher

I have a dread of weight-watchers and calorie-counters, especially at large dining tables or on occasions when everyone else is looking forward to a good tuck-in. It's positively dispiriting to eat with someone who says hold the cheese in the pizza or no dressing in my salad, please. And those who look at the cheesecake longingly and then say, `Oh, no, I really shouldn't'.

Good for their self-restraint, is all I can think of saying. But there are, of course, times when you have to come up with a recipe that will please even the keenest weight-watcher and still taste good.

This recipe for a date and walnut loaf which I found in a very old issue of *Women's Own* magazine fits the bill. It has only a smidgen of butter and still tastes fab. And if you aren't weight watching you can make it even better by slathering the slices with butter.

Date and Walnut Bread

175 gm dates
1 tsp soda bicarbonate
225 gm flour
A pinch of salt
3 tbsp golden syrup (if unavailable, substitute with honey)
25 gm butter
1 egg, beaten
50 g walnuts, chopped

Chop the dates and put in a bowl with the soda bicarbonate and pour 150 ml boiling water over. Leave to soak while you work on the other ingredients.

Sift the flour and salt into a bowl. In another bowl, cream the golden syrup and butter together. Beat the egg into the mixture. Add the nuts, the flour and the date mixture. Stir well.

Pour into a 500 gm loaf tin and bake at 170°C/325°F/Gas Mark 3 for 40 minutes or till a toothpick inserted into the loaf comes out clean. Allow to cool, before slicing and serving. If you are not watching your calories, these slices are delightful, buttered.

Makes 8 to 10 slices

97 Lightness of Being

We called these kisses when we were little and they were big, pink, airy things. Macaroons are a close cousin. Paris is, of course, home of the macaroon, with the debate raging on whether Laduree or Pierre Herme is the contender for best macaroon maker crown. The colours, the flavours, the packaging are all talking points. If you happen to be in Paris, you must make a visit to one of these two famous macaroon stores.

And now I see them in restaurants here, chic and stylish, in all manner of shades from pistachio green to lavender. The pastry chefs at Caperberry, the modern European restaurant run by Abhijit Saha, make some very nice macaroons. And Abhijit serves these at special events, high teas and even gives them away to special guests.

Looking at all the legend surrounding macaroons it would seem like they are virtually impossible for the home cook to get right. Not so. If you take a little care and follow the right recipe you can certainly make an impressive batch. Mine is a simple meringue, I don't use the ground almonds that Parisian macaroons include.

Meringues

Whites of 3 large eggs
225 gm soft caster sugar

Ensure the bowl you are mixing the eggs in is completely grease-free. Put the egg whites and sugar into the bowl and place over a larger bowl of gently simmering water. Stir till the sugar is dissolved and the whites are warm to the touch.

Remove from heat and beat with an electric whisk till the whites are cold, glossy and stiff. This will take about 15 minutes.

Preheat the oven to 150°C/300°F/Gas Mark 4. Line a baking tray with non-stick baking parchment. Put spoonfuls of the egg white mixture on to the tray and shape into discs. Use up all the mixture. Bake for 15 minutes. Then turn off the oven and allow to sit for a few hours to dry out.

Remove gently and serve sandwiched with fruit compote, chocolate or butter cream.

Makes about 24 meringues

98 Wow Them with Dessert

When I was little, cheesecake in Colombo was a small tartlet with a frangipane filling and a cashew nut embedded on the surface. Don't ask me why it was called a cheesecake.

My introduction to cheesecake made with cream cheese was in Australia where the Sara Lee dessert was a popular pudding. And I fell in love with the stuff – from buttery, crumbly base, through the sharp, creamy core and fruity topping. But a cheesecake gone wrong is a ghastly thing. Restaurants will put in way too much gelatine and call a sort of cold mousse or soufflé a cheesecake. Not done.

The genuine article, the New York-style cheesecake, needs Philadelphia cream cheese and that is expensive stuff. I know of home cooks who use everything from hung yogurt to cottage cheese to make cheesecakes.

Mine is an unconventional, but very successful cheesecake that uses, surprise, surprise, condensed milk. Topped with some fresh fruit, it's a very nice party piece.

Cheesecake

175 gm ginger biscuits or digestive biscuits
50 gm butter, melted
4 large limes
2 cans (400 gm) condensed milk
500 ml thick cream

Lightly brush a spring release tin and line with paper. Crush the biscuits and add melted butter to the crumbs. Mix thoroughly and press into the base of the tin and chill for an hour.

Grate the zest of the limes and squeeze the juice. Put the condensed milk into a large bowl and slowly whisk in the cream. Continue whisking and add the lime zest and juice.

The mixture will thicken dramatically. Pour it over the biscuit base and chill for 12 hours at least. Slice and serve. Top with a fruit compote if you like.

Serves 6-8

99 A Sweet Ending

I see my mother now, surveying her table set with fine Noritake and laden with dishes – string hopper biryani, hoppers or appam being turned out from two stove-tops, a dark, spicy chicken curry, potatoes cooked in coconut milk, sometimes brinjals in a spice paste, small fish cutlets and a variety of sambols and relishes. If the table was beautifully laid, she herself would be impeccably turned out, giving no indication of the hours spent cooking this feast.

Dinner parties of this sort were frequent at my place, for my father was keen to lavish hospitality on the diplomat and journalist friends he met in the course of reporting on foreign affairs. My mother, demure and quiet in company, but with a striking personality, may not have participated in the debates on the future of the Gaza Strip or the outcome of the Camp David summit (these were hot topics of the day), but she ensured a great evening for all her guests, with her warm hospitality and superlative food.

The response of Martin Walker, then a foreign correspondent who went on to become the editor of the Guardian, to one of my mother's dinners is still remembered in my family. It was a meal of hoppers and searing hot sambol. At the end of it, the Englishman, his cheeks flushed and his eyes watering from the spice, kissed my mom's hands repeatedly while she blushed and giggled like a teenager.

The dinners would invariably end with a gargantuan dessert. A tropical fruit salad with fresh pineapple, papaya, mangoes and bananas and moistened with sugar syrup was often tossed up. The watalappam was another dessert of choice at my mother's dinner parties.

This dessert of Malay origin is a heavenly balance of three simple ingredients – coconut milk, eggs and jaggery; not any jaggery, but the one from the palm or kitul tree as it's known in Sri Lanka.

Watalappam always reminds me of my mother's capacity, passion and enthusiasm for cooking and feeding people – not just special guests, but everyone who walked into her home. I miss her and I thank her for the legacy she has left me.

Watalappam

4 cups freshly squeezed coconut milk
500 gm jaggery
10 eggs, beaten
1 tsp vanilla or
6 cardamoms, husked and seeds crushed

Place the coconut milk in a large pan.

Grate or roughly break up the jaggery and add it to the coconut milk. Warm gently over a low heat till the jaggery is dissolved. Turn off the heat. Add the eggs to the coconut milk and jaggery mixture. Add the vanilla or cardamom powder.

Strain the mixture into the bowl in which the pudding is to be steamed. Cover it with foil. Place in a pressure cooker and steam for 30 minutes, without using the weight. The watalappam should have set like a firm custard. Serve warm or chilled.

If you can't get kitul jaggery, use patali gur or Kerala palm jaggery; but the latter is often very gritty and needs to be melted and strained before use.

Serves 10